*I'm left with a kaleidoscopic impressi[...]
story, with parallels and motifs that
gradual revelation of one cleverly-imagined solution to an age old*
mystery. **Rebecca Tope***(author of 19 murder-mystery books
and ghost writer of the novels 'Rosemary and Thyme')*

*Who was the real Shakespeare? This intriguing story is full of
surprises and is beautifully written in modern and Elizabethan
English. The author brings together a few eccentric old academics and
weaves her tale round their past love affairs, their ambitions,
rivalries, secrets and failures. I strongly recommend this book.*
Susan Skinner

*Mandy Pannett draws the threads – those of long-burning rivalry,
those of passion and jealousy – from both modern academic circles
and from the 16th century of Shakespeare's world. She weaves them
together into an intriguing tapestry, spices them with historical
revelation and a cry for recognition from long-hidden descendants.
Finally she draws the threads together for the finale, reminds us that
'All the world's a stage' and in masterful delivery makes you pleased,
that just for a while, we watched the players on an intricate stage."*
Douglas Pugh

*This is not just another 'who was Shakespeare' book. It is a novel
that works on several levels, telling stories of ambition, intrigue and
greed, love, sacrifice and loss within a beautifully structured
framework. The author moves with uncanny ease back and forth
between the 20th and the 16th centuries; this is due to her love of
history and accurate research but also to crisp narration and an
ability to make what is imagined (often in real settings) very tangible
for the reader.* **Pansy Maurer-Alvarez** *(Dolores: The Alpine
Years and 'When The Body Says It's Leaving.)*

In The Onion Stone Mandy Pannett has written an extraordinary story. The plot gathers pace with an interweaving of the sixteenth and twentieth centuries as intricate as the knotwork that she creates in the lives of the protagonists, and with great scholarly knowledge she draws us into a tale of intrigue, counter-intrigue, treachery, love, rivalry, loss – and questions about the identity of the greatest playwright England has known (but possible answers do not alight on the usual suspects). The author's ear for language is perfectly attuned to the Elizabethan era. When I came to the end I wasn't sure what was fact and what was fiction; but I knew that all of it was intelligent and gripping. This is a rich and wide-ranging read, much bigger than its length in terms of pages. **Roselle Angwin** *(Imago 2011,Bardo 2011)*

The Onion Stone

The Onion Stone

Mandy

Pannett

Published by
Pewter Rose Press
17 Mellors Rd,
West Bridgford
Nottingham, NG2 6EY
United Kingdom
www.pewter-rose-press.com

First published in Great Britain 2011
© Mandy Pannett 2011
ISBN 978-1-908136-0-15

The right of Mandy Pannett to be identified as author of this work has been asserted by her in accordance with the Copyright, Designs and Patents Act 1988

British Library Cataloguing in Publication Data
A catalogue record for this book is available from the British Library

All characters appearing in this work are fictitious. Any resemblance to real persons, living or dead, is purely coincidental.

Cover design by www.thedesigndepot.co.uk
Printed and bound in Great Britain

ACKNOWLEDGMENTS

This book is for my friend Jane Biggs and in memory of dear Colin.

Special thanks to the following people:
Anne and Nick McDonnell of Pewter Rose Press who have made this possible.
Becky, Diana, Doug, Eilidh, Kate, Krystyna, Michelle, Nikki, Pansy, Roselle, Susan and many other generous friends and writing groups for all their advice and encouragement.
Members of 'The Write Idea' and 'Fiction Forge' for their interest and support.
Last, but never least, my lovely family.

THE ONION STONE

From '*The Bishop orders his tomb at St Praxed's Church*' by
Robert Browning

What's done is done, and she is dead beside,
Dead long ago and I am Bishop since
… And so, about this tomb of mine. I fought
With tooth and nail to save my niche, ye know.
— Old Gandalf cozened me, despite my care,
… Old Gandalf with his paltry onion-stone,
Put me where I may look at him!
And no more lapis to delight the world!
… And leave me in my church, the church for peace,
That I may watch, at leisure if he leers —
Old Gandalf — at me, from his onion-stone,
As still he envied me, so fair she was!

*Onion Stone — a type of marble with a layered effect

'STILL HE ENVIED ME'

The summer began peacefully enough. On the Avon swans glided by to the approval of tourists, at Cambridge the students of the eighties sighed in the heat of examination rooms and in West Sussex, Rupert David Davendish placed this advert in an academic journal:

Academic research and secretarial assistance required for work on Shakespearian sources.
Enquiries and details to R. D. Davendish at the address below.

"What research is that, Ardie?" asked Frances Goodbody, the author's wife. She peered at the advert, pushing wisps of hair off her face. "Do you mean to say poor old Shakespeare's still got some bones to rattle? I thought you and Ellis had picked him clean between you."

"Don't mention Ellis to me," said her husband. "How you can even talk about that lunatic, that windbag, that ... that ... overbearing, pompous old crank in the same breath as me, I don't know!" He breathed heavily, red faced.

"Don't excite yourself, Ardie," said Frances gently. "You know it's not good for you. As for Ellis, I daresay he thinks the same about you. He's always on TV calling you the crank and windbag. It doesn't mean anything. It's time you both made peace. We ought to invite him to dinner sometime. You don't need to mention Shakespeare," she added, seeing her husband's face. "Shakespeare will be taboo. Strictly forbidden.

We could all talk about Victorian poets. There are one or two things I'd like to ask Ellis. About Browning's onion stone, for instance, in 'The Bishop Orders his Tomb.' I think there's quite a similarity between the two old rivals and you and Ellis. Have you ever noticed it yourself …?"

"Frances," said her husband, "you drive me mad with your stupid remarks! Prattling away to yourself all day long. I think you're going round the bend and taking me with you! Heaven knows I've more important things to do than stand here all day. I've got research to do, you know. That's why I need a secretary!" He groped for the door handle, stumbling out. "Get back to your Browning."

Frances clenched her fists. "You need a secretary, you foolish old man, because you can't see your nose in front of your face any more!" She sighed. "Get back to Browning? No, not today, my old love. I've got much better things to write about." She smiled to herself and headed towards her study.

R. D. Davendish, known to his wife and few close friends as Ardie, was a proud man. Proud of being a celebrity, an expert on Shakespeare, and even prouder of his reputation as an eccentric. This he went out of his way to cultivate. Over the years his long-suffering wife watched him transform from a brilliant young man with a quick temper and a passionate desire to change the world, into a bad-tempered, obstinate old crank. No other word for it; Ardie had become a crank. All very well for the outside world to applaud every outrageous remark as he joyfully cut some so-called expert down to size. All very well for the Press to devote column after column to each cock-eyed theory as Ardie uncovered, yet again, the identity of The Dark Lady or discovered a new cipher or anagram, written in Latin, in the last scene of Timon of Athens. Frances was his wife and she had to live with him.

They had been married a long time. An interesting match that excited the academic and social world of Cambridge in its time: the beautiful, young student who everyone said was 'going somewhere' and the brilliant Shakespearian scholar who, like a firework, was on his way up. To the very top. Somewhere along the way, the plan changed. If there had ever been a plan. Ardie had reached the top alright and was still fizzing around frenetically on its border, but something had happened to Frances. As her husband grew larger than life, she became quiet and secretive. A shadowy figure in a dusty-grey kind of way, Frances Goodbody, the toast of the town, had quietly withdrawn from the arena. She, who could have taken her pick from any number of bright young academics, chose Ardie and faded.

Now she had a much older husband to contend with: a silent, daily battle that took all her energies and wit. Ardie to placate and keep on an even keel so that his blood pressure didn't soar alarmingly more than once a week; Ardie to restrain, without his knowing it, so that he didn't go over-stepping the mark, offending the academic world once too often; Ardie's image of himself to be soothed and protected and polished up whenever it grew tarnished. On a simple daily basis, there was Ardie to feed.

"I'm not a fussy man," he would insist. "Bread and butter and a slab of cheese is all I ask. I'd live on that. Nothing simpler."

"Yes," said Frances, "but the bread has to come from the baker's at the very top of the High Street and the cheese from that little shop in Petworth and nowhere else. I don't call that simple! For all your talk about bread and cheese, you know that's not true. You look forward to your meals and like them on time, even though you are always late!"

Ardie picked up a book and consulted the index, ignoring her as he did any form of criticism.

Four days after the advert was placed there was a batch of letters.

"You sort them out, Frances, read me some," said Ardie, sipping his early morning tea in the garden as pale sunshine flickered through the trees. Already the early June day promised to be hot. "See if there's anyone with a modicum of intelligence in that lot."

"Anyone who could put up with you for more than one day you mean," said Frances, lazily opening envelopes.

Her husband looked indignant. "What are you talking about? There must be dozens of people who would give their right arm for the chance to work with me."

"Quite right, dear," said Frances. "Oh look, there's an application here from someone called Henry Shakspeare. What a coincidence. I wonder if he's a descendant of your Bard."

Ardie glanced irritably at the letter. "Don't be ridiculous, Frances. There aren't any left."

His wife gave him a strange look. "I do know that, my love. I was only teasing you. I haven't lived with you all these years without knowing the facts and theories inside out. I'm nearly as obsessed with the wretched man as you and Ellis, if such a thing is possible."

Frances continued with the letters, reading bits out, placing them in piles. She gave a start, glanced at her husband, and slipped an envelope under her saucer.

"Mind you," said her husband slowly, "there might be a family connection somewhere, though I thought I knew them all. It's an unusual spelling of the name. Write to him, Frances, and tell him to come for an interview. Frances, stop woolgathering. Are you listening? Write to him."

"What?" said his wife. "Write to who?"

"To that fellow we spoke about. The Shakespeare one."

"Oh right," said Frances, hunting through the pile for Henry Shakspeare's letter and skimming through it. "He sounds quite reasonable. A Cambridge man. That should please you. I'll write to him straight away."

She stood up, carefully balancing cups and saucers.

"By the way, my dear," said her husband softly, "aren't you going to read me that other letter as well?"

"What other letter?" she said, moving in the direction of the house.

"The one you are hiding under the teacups. The one I assume, judging from your guilty and clumsy manner, to be from T. Townsend Ellis. Unless you have a secret admirer."

He chuckled to himself, licking chocolate off his fingers. "At your age, my dear, I would imagine that to be highly unlikely."

Frances studied her husband's forehead, as if selecting a target point.

"It is from Ellis. His handwriting is unmistakeable. I'm only hiding the letter, as you put it, because you are so paranoiac about him."

A dragonfly glittered and darted over the lily leaves on the pond. In a nearby garden a child was crying: a long wailing sound.

"Aren't you going to read it then?" said Ardie.

"You know," said Frances, as if he hadn't spoken, "I am not sure I like that remark about me being too old to have an admirer. I may be ancient, Ardie, but I am still younger than you. In case you have forgotten."

"I haven't forgotten," said her husband. "It's not something you let me forget. And I was only joking. You think I don't appreciate you, but I do." His eyes brightened. "Remember how envious Ellis was when you chose me and not him? I was always the one that got the girls, you know."

"Well," said Frances, "it was a very long time ago and we are all old now."

Her husband nodded. "He was mad with envy though. Didn't like me stealing a march on him. Who knows, maybe I can still get the better of him, for all that I am as old as the hills as you remind me. There's still time. Plenty of time. Now read me what the old bluffer has to say."

FROM THE NOTEBOOK OF GILBERT SHAKESPEARE

JUNE 1588

Seventeen summers gone since that day and my memories as fresh as though but a moment ago. How cold my bones were and aching, with my heart's blood thumping in my ears as I crouched there, cramped and battered like a small, twisted shell. Slowly I opened my eyes, peering at the candles still flickering in the grey half light. My throat was burning with fear. A sudden breeze made the flames quiver and as I started up in panic a gilded dragon came rippling towards me from the tapestry, spitting fire, devouring me with blood red eyes. As I screamed and screamed in the empty chamber and fell sobbing to my knees, the dragon came thundering down upon me. I knew I was surely in hell.

The room was sweet with the scent of gillyflowers and a gentle sun warmed my face. Far away someone was whispering to me, fainter than an echo, whispering that I was safe, that the nightmare was over, that I was home. I feared to break the spell and muttered feebly, feigning sleep.

"How is the child?" said a man's voice, and I opened my eyes in terror and felt fear thudding through my veins.

"Hush now," whispered a girl close to me. "Poor little boy, no need to be afraid."

Frantically I reached out and grabbed her hand and she smiled at me then and through my panic and my grief I saw her face.

Tannakin, Tannakin. Seventeen summers gone since I first saw you. Oh Anne, my own Tannakin, how can I bear my loss?

And so, as I begin to write, it all returns to me. Come now my traitor pen, the facts, the facts. Write down the facts. That way the winding sheet and worms can gain no hold. In that April of 1571 I was taken in as a tumbling boy, at my Lady Anne's request, into the household of William Cecil, my Lord Burghley, the most feared and famous man in the land. How I came to be there, cast out and cursed as a monster, as a deformity in God's sight at the age of seven years, sent away from my mother's arms by those who knew best, or thought they did, to be a vagabond or to make my fortune if the fates so chose — how this came about and how I came to be alone and screaming in my Lord Burghley's London home on that April morning and how he then gave me as a gift to his daughter Anne — all these facts are well known and recorded so many times over that to rehearse them again would be but idle. In truth, Dame Gossip has no need to play inventor with my early years.

Suffice to say that those months from April to December were full of joy, as bright as the roses in my Lord's garden where my Lady Anne Cecil walked with me at her heels, her tumbling boy, her Gillyflower as she called me, making sweet mockery of my name Gilbert. Sometimes she was serious and dignified as befitted a betrothed lady and the daughter of Her Majesty's chief minister. On days like these we would walk for an hour, her with a volume of Greek, brow creased in concentration, and me, two steps behind, playing games with her shadow. But then she would toss the book away and darting round catch hold of me, spinning me round and round as though I were a baby or a toy — for that was how she saw me then though all things change — and no matter that she was the daughter of Lord Burghley and betrothed to Edward de Vere, the Earl of Oxford, she was but thirteen years and with a heart made for the summer sun.

'TO SAVE MY NICHE'

"Right," said Ardie to Henry Shakspeare as they stood in the hallway, "let's show you your room and then we'll have a quick walk round the town, so you can get your bearings, and then we'll get to work." His eyes sparkled. "I can't wait to hear about this evidence you mentioned on the phone. From what you hinted when we talked … the documents you've got …" He looked hopefully at the cases and bags that had arrived with his new assistant. "Have you brought the originals with you? I've got a safe. Perhaps they'd better go in there?"

Henry laughed, not pleasantly. "No, they're locked away in a bank vault in London. I'm no fool."

Frances, silent as a whisper behind her husband, studied the two men. Ardie, frowning and muttering to himself to hide his embarrassment, picked up Henry's bags and stumbled towards the stairs. The younger man watched him, a mocking look in his dark eyes, and slowly traced his finger over a livid, strawberry-red birthmark that blotched his left cheek and the corner of his lips. Although Frances knew from his letter that he was thirty-two years old, he had the appearance of a younger man: thin and wiry with an intense, nervous energy.

"I don't like him," thought Frances. "I wish he hadn't come." She shivered and at that moment Henry stepped forward.

"Let me do that, Mr Davendish," he said, moving lightly ahead of the old man up the stairs. "You mustn't wait on me. Show me my room and I'll get rid of these and then, as you say, we can get to work."

He turned and smiled down at Ardie. For an instant the smile lit up his whole face.

"Where's that woman gone?" muttered Ardie, peering round crossly. "Oh there you are, Frances, lurking in the shadows as usual. Show Henry to his room, can't you! I'll be in my study if anyone wants me."

He shoved his way downstairs and into his room, slamming the door. Across the hallway, Henry and Ardie's wife studied each other.

Ten minutes later Frances, who was chopping up spring onions and hard boiled eggs on the pine table in the kitchen, put down her knife and headed in the direction of Ardie's study. Only one way to satisfy her curiosity, she thought. Tapping loudly on the door out of habit, she went straight in, knowing her husband, hard of hearing these days, wouldn't hear her.

Both Frances and Ardie, as authors in their own right, had individual studies. Frances's room was small and tidy with a large bowl of poppies on her desk by the window and no sign of papers anywhere. Ardie's room was sprawling and messy, covered from floor to ceiling with books and more books and with manuscripts, journals, letters and newspaper cuttings piled up on tables and chairs and tumbling onto the floor. Ardie had several times been filmed and interviewed in this study; one of the Sunday magazines had done a whole article on the room as an author's work base. He himself had been photographed, sitting comfortably in his old leather armchair, puffing on a pipe and glancing casually through the collected works of Shakespeare. At the time Frances thought it an ill-chosen image for her irascible, hyperactive husband but kept quiet. Ardie was proud of the article.

"Pity they didn't mention me," Frances had said. "I'd have made a good photo, creeping around in the background with duster in one hand and notebook in the other."

Ardie had ignored her. These days he ignored everything to do with Frances or anyone else.

"What do you want?" he demanded, heaving himself out of the armchair as his wife walked into the room. "I thought I said I didn't want to be disturbed."

"No, dear," she replied, "you said you'd be in your study if anyone wanted you." He glared at her irritably and began to pace up and down.

"It so happens," continued Frances, standing in front of her husband so he had to stop, "that I do want you. I need some information, Ardie." This had the effect of making him look at her, Ardie being unable to resist appeals for information. "I need to know a few things about Mr Henry Shakspeare. Not the facts, I can read those for myself in his CV, but about this phone call that made you so excited. What is this evidence he's offering you? Is there something totally new about Shakespeare? Something no-one knows about? You've got to tell me Ardie, otherwise I might say the wrong thing. You know, my love, it won't kill you to share a snippet of information with me. I can see it's bottled up inside you. Just give me a hint."

Ardie took a deep breath, torn between inclination to ignore his wife as he would a buzzing fly and the longing to share the secret that was bursting inside him.

"I'll tell you this much, Frances," he said finally, "though I don't see why I should." His eyes brightened. "Henry Shakspeare claims to be a descendant of the author." He stepped closer to his wife. "The real author I mean. He claims it wasn't William Shakespeare who wrote the plays but his brother Gilbert. He's got proof, Frances, pages and pages of proof!" He stepped back and stared at his wife triumphantly. "That's all I'm telling you. You'll find out the rest when you type up the notes for my book."

A thousand doubts and questions burned inside Frances's head but she dared not ask any of them. She turned to go out of the room.

"Frances," said her husband.

"Yes? What's the matter, Ardie? Why are you looking at me like that?"

"You do realise, Frances, that this is the most exciting thing that has ever happened to me? This is my big chance, my last chance if you like, to … pick the winning number … to come up with the prize. This could be the scoop of the century, the true identity of Shakespeare revealed at last, turning out to be none of the big-name claimants but William's own nonentity of a brother — and if you so much as breathe a word to that bigot, that fraud, that fool Ellis, I'll kill you with my bare hands!" He stopped, gasping.

"Ardie," said Frances, with tears in her eyes, "if you don't stop getting so agitated it'll be yourself you'll kill!"

She hurried out, back to the kitchen.

"Dear God," she said, as she chopped the onions viciously, "let it happen this time. Let it be true!"

Later, after a meal and strained conversation, they all went for a walk. Midhurst, where Ardie and Frances had made their home since leaving Cambridge several years before, was at its best in the mid-June evening. The house where they lived was shabby but comfortable, overlooking a large, walled garden at the back, although the front door itself opened almost directly onto the busy, half-cobbled, main street.

"That's why we chose it," said Ardie, when Henry expressed an interest. "I like to think we've got the best of both worlds. At the back it's peaceful, secluded, quite idyllic — what Frances calls 'chocolate boxy.' But here at the front, it's another world. Man on the move. Lorries and cars under your feet. Literally. Even on top of them if you're not careful! There's the local fish and chippery." He pointed to a shop enticingly named The Tasty Plaice. "Good, isn't it? Right next to the Funeral Parlour. Remember that, Henry. Could be useful if you fancy dropping down dead over a plate of haddock and peas. You won't have far to go." He chuckled at his own joke.

They walked on up the street, Ardie in a witty mood and humming softly to himself, the others silent. In the church of St Mary Magdalene and St Denys the light was still on.

"Look at this," said Henry after they had wandered round for several minutes. He was standing in front of a large memorial tablet, peering at the writing. "It's commemorating a

24

father and his two sons who served in the church choir for sixty years. Sixty years!"

"What's wrong with that?" said Ardie, coming up behind him and staring at the memorial which he had never noticed before. "A very good thing to do. They had some first class choirs at King's in my day. Best in the land. Still are. We always listen to the Christmas Eve service on the radio. Takes us back to the old days."

"Yes, but sixty years!" repeated Henry. "It's a lifetime!"

"You needn't scoff, my love," said Frances to her husband. "Mr Shakspeare is obviously horrified at the thought of the monotony, the repetition. You must admit you'd die of boredom as well, doing the same thing for sixty years. That is," she added, glancing challengingly at Henry, "unless it's hunting for Shakespeare."

She moved across to study a nearby brass inscription. Ardie wandered slowly in the direction of the main door.

"This is my favourite one," she said. "Come and see what you make of it, Mr Shakspeare."

He moved over to the memorial and for a moment their two heads, one grey and one dark, were side by side as they studied the words in the light slanting from the stained glass window.

"'In loving memory of St John Dacres Montgomery Campbell,'" Henry read aloud. "Good grief, what a name. '2nd Lieutenant York and Lancaster Regiment. Killed by a fall on Mardah Mountain, Baluchistan.'" He peered at the words again. "Where on earth is Baluchistan, Mrs Davendish?"

"I'm not sure," she said. "By the way, my name is Frances Goodbody. My professional name. I'm an author too. Several books on Robert Browning, a couple on Keats and ... and I write other things as well."

Henry stared at her, startled.

"Please go on," she said. "Read the rest of the inscription."

"Oh yes. Right. Where was I? 'Killed by ... Baluchistan. 26th June 1908. Aged twenty-two and a half years. His warfare is accomplished.'" He studied the memorial in silence. Frances waited expectantly.

"Yes," he said slowly, fingering the birthmark on his face. "Think I can see why it's your favourite. Think I've got it. Is it the half bit?"

"It was important to someone," said Frances gently. "Probably his mother." She looked round anxiously. "I think we had better go and find my husband. He gets a bit of a chip on his shoulder if he feels left out of things."

Together they hurried out of the church in search of Ardie.

LETTER FROM AN UNKNOWN NOBLEMAN TO A FRIEND

NOVEMBER 1571

And so my good friend I take up my pen as promised upon my returning full wearily from Cecil House where I have passed these several days. And though I know you be eager of news to cheer you in your adversity and wait upon my account most hopefully, I fear no jewelled words spring sparkling to my pen, for I tell you my eyes burn with such weariness and my poor head hurts with such a surfeit of learned conversation, that I think my words shall trickle slower than sand in a time glass.

My Lord Burghley keeps a most spacious house, teeming with more activity than a river at height of salmon spawning. And though the house be furnished most finely and my eyes grew dazzled from such a wealth of portraits, plate and statues, yet it is a sombre household, with no private company of actors to ease the brain and no musicians at mealtimes to help the digestion, for my Lord William prefers conversation — not of politics for he puts aside his Secretary's duties when at home — but of science and history and antiquities and theology and classics and other such subjects. In truth my friend my very brain did ache, but if you would meet with my Lord and creep into his favour, then you must act the man of many parts but the wise scholar most of all.

What of my Lord Burghley himself you ask, for I know how in your enforced idleness you long for news, snatching at whispers like a brigand at a purse though it contain no gems. You demand what truth in tales of spies and intrigue, of secret informers plotting in the dark of midnight and sudden murder where the assassin's blade flashes and the shadows are full of death. My friend, it seems to me my Lord is as a man with a mask which none may see behind and, for all I know, every tapestry held a spy lurking behind its golden threads, but I saw none. You know how, in secret, men name him The Fox and indeed, when long shadows fell over the table and all were in their cups, weary and stumbling save only him, he did seem so to me — a cunning fox with stealthy ways, swift to pounce and silent in his killing. A man whose enemy I would not be. I am growing weary and the room full of shadows ...

Now is the day bright and I, much refreshed with slumber, take up my pen again, the demons of the night being now laid to rest with the shades that gave them form.

What else can I tell to feed your mind, eager as I know it is for scandal and for gossip? Now do not turn on me in anger for I do but jest. If Madam Gossip can restore you to the favour you so crave, then I will squeeze the ugly wench until she shrieks. As for scandal concerning my Lord Burghley, there is none nor has been since his youthful days when he dallied with one Mary Clarke, whose mother kept an ale house, and with a boldness and a passion now unknown to the Queen's most mighty Secretary of State, he did insist upon a marriage with no dowry. God and his angels must have favoured him for she died most fortunately soon after, leaving my Lord with a son. Since then my Lady Mildred has been in dominance more absolute than the Tartar.

I know you would have me here describe my Lady but in truth I cannot for she did make me shake in my shoes so that I scarce could meet her eye. A formidable lady who is accounted one of the most learned women of the land, an equal to our own fair Queen if such be possible, for she speaks Greek as smoothly as her own tongue. She is a wife no doubt most fitted for the high and mighty Lord William, but a wife I think not fitted for the warmer hours. For my part I would as soon spend one hour with Bess of Southwark Bridge — though her kisses reek of sack and garlic and my member boils and burns and oozes with the devil's pus for many a week — than a lifetime in Lady Mildred's bed where her cold breath would freeze a man's blood to icicles. She is a death's head my friend, and there are better ways of dying.

The gentler moments, if such a man as my Lord William Cecil can know of tenderness and sweetness, are spent with his daughter Anne who he calls Tannakin, a foolish name. She is but a child, a pretty thing, on whose face shadows and smiles take their turn to dance like butterflies. A changeling of a child I think, for in her I see as yet no trace of him. Or of her learned mother. I watched her in an idle moment from my chamber window, laughing and playing with a tiny tumbling boy on whom she dotes and who scrambles in her footsteps like a fawning, whining cur. I fear too soon all smiles will fade for she is betrothed to Edward de Vere, the young Earl of Oxford and the ceremony next month. Her eyes are full of stars and he is handsome, bold and strong. A man of influence, perhaps, if you were so inclined to gain his ear. I fear that he will break her heart within the year, for he is vicious, so men say, degenerate too, taking his pleasure where he may, be it boy or wench he cares not. Then will he discard the object of his lust, like tainted meat.

These are cruel times, my friend, as you know and I am in doubt how best to advise you to regain the favour of our sovereign lady. Informers are everywhere and there are none who may be trusted. These careless words I write for your amusement and consolation could cost me my head if they should fall into the wrong hands. Burn this letter upon the receipt I beg of you. Oh my friend, if there be such treachery in high places, what hope for you and me? I tell you one thing more, he …

'THIS TOMB OF MINE'

T. Townsend Ellis fetched a dustpan and brush from the cupboard under the stairs, firmly brushed the caterpillar droppings off the window ledge and contemplated the jagged edges of the leaves on his yucca plant. No doubt about it, some predator was chewing its way through the plant. One morning he would come downstairs and there would be the yucca, solid and stiff as a cactus, stripped to the stem by a caterpillar with jaws like death. He studied the plant thoughtfully, then, careful not to scatter any soil on the soft beige carpet, walked to the cupboard outside the front door, lifted the lid off the dustbin and lowered the whole plant inside.

As he replaced the lid, sealing both yucca and caterpillar in darkness, a picture flickered behind his eyes of Sandra the Spider who had lived in his rooms at Cambridge in what seemed centuries ago. He remembered Frances Goodbody arriving at his door with rain in her hair at the very moment when he was about to sweep Sandra, her offspring and all her cobwebs into oblivion. It occurred to him he had been standing with a dustpan and brush in his hand on that occasion too.

Thanks to Frances, Sandra had been saved to weave many a tangled web in the tall, dark corners of his room. He toyed briefly with an image of a later student, sweating away in the rooms that had once been his, too dull to notice the cobwebs in the corner, but then dismissed the idea as idle fancy. These days Ellis did not believe in wasting time on idle fancy. Gone

31

were the days when a girl with rain in her hair could move him.

He shook his head to clear it and walked briskly over to his writing desk. There was work to be done and letters to be written and posted. Ellis was a man much in demand. A busy man. For a start he needed to write to the producer of the current Media in the Arts:

Dear Paul

Good to hear from you. Yes, I will be delighted to take part in your forum on the relevance of Shakespeare in this century. Perhaps you will let me know more details nearer the time. Who else will be involved by the way? I believe R. D. Davendish is out of the country at present and, in any case, I am not sure he would have anything relevant to add on the subject of relevance.

Ellis chuckled as he wrote this, admiring his own wit. He knew Ardie wasn't abroad, but was getting tired of meeting him on every discussion programme. Great for the organisers, they could be sure of a sparring match and the media loved it, but Ellis was growing bored. It was time to end the double act. It had gone on too long. Fifty years too long. It was time Ardie retired from the scene.

Carefully he added his signature. Not for the first time he considered the complexities of his name. T. Townsend Ellis, known simply as Ellis to his acquaintances, often wished he had been consulted in the early stages. He had been christened Timothy Townsend by a mother with a taste for the whimsical, but had rebelled from an early age. He'd managed to drop the Timothy bit successfully, defying its resurrection and retaining only the initial T. That still did not prevent Frances, in a teasing mood, from addressing him as Timmy, like an Enid Blyton dog; or Ardie, in fine form, referring to him on television as 'Tee Tee' Ellis. He shivered and the mist outside the window crept through the shutters into the room. Those two — Frances and Ardie — the very thought of them hurt like splinters.

Reminded of Ardie, Ellis searched for the strange letter he had received a few days earlier and re-read it slowly:

Dear Professor Ellis

I am currently employed as a research assistant to Professor R. D. Davendish. I have, in my possession, a great many documents relating to the authorship of Shakespeare and am working closely with the Professor on establishing their authenticity. While these documents are highly confidential and I am not, at present, in a position to share their contents with anyone except Professor Davendish, it may be that at some time in the future I will need to consult you on one or two of the documents. It is, as yet, too early to tell.

How the originals of these letters and journals came into my possession is immaterial but I can assure you my ownership of them is totally legitimate. I am writing merely to 'put you in the picture,' as it were, to inform you of their existence. There is no need to reply to this letter. I will contact you if, and when, the occasion requires.

Yours sincerely
Henry Shakspeare

This letter had caused Ellis some agitation when he first read it and he could feel his heart beating faster as he studied it again. His first reaction had been one of fury.

"The sheer impertinence of it," he had muttered as he pushed the letter violently across his desk. "Who does he think he is? Him and his stupid, secret documents that he might, or might not, consult me about!"

But later, as he thought about it, he had become intrigued.

'What does he mean?' he wondered. 'What has Ardie got hold of?'

This was the worrying part. Henry Shakspeare would probably turn out to be a crank with a wild cock and bull story and Ardie would, yet again, be caught with egg on his face. With a bit of luck.

'But what if he's on to something …' Ellis, re-reading the letter on this misty day in August, was a worried man.

Later that day, after a light lunch, Ellis threw his dark-blue overcoat over his shoulders like a cape and set off for his customary daily walk in Greenwich Park. An earlier mist had lifted and the July day was bright and sunny, children were running up the steep hill and rolling down again, laughing and shouting. The river sparkled in the sunshine and people sat watching the boats, enjoying their own or another's company. Ellis saw none of this. His thoughts were heavy and he walked along as one in a trance. Frances had told him, on more than one occasion, that it was a total waste for him to live in an ancient and historic place like Greenwich since he was unaware of his surroundings most of the time. Where

Frances could gaze around and imagine the world of kings and queens, of Elizabeth with her processions and tournaments and hunts and royal barges on the river, Ellis saw none of it.

An intense, complex, reserved man who lived most of his life in the world of books, he felt himself slowly come to life in the Sixties and Seventies with the advent of hi-tech. Ellis liked the world of the media. It expressed him, developed him, spoke for him and fulfilled him. The man of scholarship and reserve had grown to love being public property.

At the top of the hill Ellis stopped to post his letters. As well as the forum on Shakespeare there had been an invitation to be present, the following month, at an event which sent chills up and down his spine at the thought of it. This, a closely guarded secret, was the latest attempt to X-ray the Shakespeare Monument in the Church of the Holy Trinity at Stratford using the most advanced technology possible. Ellis had been one of the prime instigators of this deed and he shook at the thought. What if the Monument held the original manuscripts of Shakespeare's plays, long since lost? What if these manuscripts were there and proved, as Ellis and others had come to believe, that the real author of the plays was not the ill-educated man of Stratford but the brilliant, scandalous Edward de Vere, Earl of Oxford? What if Ellis should be the one to prove all this once and for all? How envious Ardie would be. It would totally destroy him. Ellis hurried home in some excitement. Next month would be a good month. There was a lot to anticipate.

And so evening fell and ended a typical day in the life of T. Townsend Ellis. He had seen no-one, spoken to no-one, barely noticed the day and yet he was not unhappy. He settled himself at his desk as shadows fell and pulled a sheaf of paper towards him. He contemplated writing to Frances to see if he could find out what Ardie was up to with the Henry Shakspeare business, but resisted the temptation. Best not to let Ardie know he knew anything, that way he might learn more. Besides, if he started corresponding with Frances, he might be tempted to boast about the Shakespeare Monument and his hopes and plans, and that would never do. If Ardie got wind of that little scheme he would cause such an uproar that he might blow the whole project sky-high. Heaven knew it had taken long enough to get permission. No, let him read about it in the newspapers and die of envy.

Ellis opened his notebook. He had work to do and now was the time to start. His old college of King's had invited him to submit a paper for the forthcoming symposium on M. R. James who was Provost of the College at the beginning of the century. Ellis knew more about M. R. James and his Victorian ghost stories than anyone else alive. He knew every one of those ghosts intimately. Even now, on the occasion of his rare visits to Cambridge, they would greet him. He'd turn round a corner and there would be one, quickly sliding out of sight, or they might appear from underneath the arches of a bridge, leaning out, hollow-eyed and leering at the fools on the river bank. Ellis knew them all. They were his shadows, always there, day and night, winter and summer. Someday, he supposed, he would come face to face with one and that would be his destiny. At least he would recognise it when it came.

As light faded he was still scribbling hard, too involved to move and turn on the light. He paused to think back to a day long ago, when he had gone with Frances to a local church to look at the inscription which M. R. James knew and used as a theme:

'Death is like a shadow which always follows the body.'

He had read it out loud and he remembered how Frances shivered and moved close to him and slipped her warm hand into his. They had gone outside and the sky and the churchyard was full of shadows and it was raining, but she pushed her wet hair back off her face and smiled provocatively up at him and he didn't notice the rain or the shadows. Ellis sighed. He picked up his pen again.

'There was one inscription that M. R. James knew well,' he wrote. 'Death is like a shadow which always follows the body.'

LETTER FROM AN ANONYMOUS OBSERVER

DECEMBER 1571

... In haste to tell you news from London where a throng of lovely ladies weep and tug their hair in rage but now are doomed to wear the willow for news is in of young Earl of Oxford's capture by the upstart Cecil clan for he, that handsome charmer of all hearts, is now betrothed to Lady Anne with plans afoot for Christmas wedding joy.

AN ACCOUNT OF THE WEDDING OF ANNE CECIL

DECEMBER 1571

... the bride, in garments all of white, was led to church by two sweet page boys and one small tumbling boy, each one with rosemary about their silken sleeves. The lady wore her long hair loose and hanging down behind. A fine bride cup of gilt and silver was carried in procession with a branch of gilded rosemary entwined with lace and ribbons of peach and tawny flame.

The Earl of Oxford and his fair Countess then journeyed on with merriment to Lord Burghley's London house for many days of feasts and celebration.

LETTER FROM THE EARL OF SUSSEX TO HIS WIFE

DECEMBER 1571

My lady

I pray with all my heart your health be good and your delivery not yet awhile until my safe return. The snow falls heavy as I pen these words but be assured I will make haste as soon as I may most courteously leave these ceremonies. You chide me for my absence, your time being so near, but my Lord Burghley did most earnestly entreat my presence at this time and I could ill refuse. Know you that my duty and concern is always yours.

You did demand on my departing that I should write most fully of my Lady Anne's wedding. Yet you must know I am but a poor man with my words and if you would have me prate in fulsome terms of silks and satins and taffetas and cambric then shall I be a poor scribe.

The Countess of Oxford, as now she is, was dressed most fine though pale as her shift and I did see her trembling, though with fear or joy I know not. I took observance, as you did ask, of the nuptial ring which was of two hands clasping a jewelled heart. The Earl of Oxford did look most fine in black and scarlet satin with silver garters.

My Lord Burghley gave his daughter many rare gifts. I did observe an inkstand of silver gilt and mother of pearl and a set of fine gold plates enamelled with birds with which the lady was much pleased. The Earl of Oxford did present his bride with a fan of swansdown and green velvet embroidered with seed pearls with a gold handle inlaid with half moons of diamonds. In faith I make a fair scribe do I not? I have taken careful note for your delight of such niceties. The Earl did also give his wife much fine jewellery. I saw a chain of agates garnished with gold which he did place around her neck. I confess I thought the chain too heavy for so delicate a lady and though she smiled and gazed at him with joy and caressed his hand as he did settle the chain, still I made note he scarce did look at her and seemed as one impatient to be done. Though he bears himself most proudly as befits his noble name, I fear he is a man of discontent and fierce of temper. I do recall how he, some years since, when a royal ward of court in Burghley's house, did run a sword through an under-cook who he said had spied on him and Lord William much concerned to claim a misadventure and so smothered up the deed.

Men say there is much enmity hidden deeper than a bee within a flower between Lord Burghley and his new son. I did also hear The Earl of Oxford say, and this dear wife you must keep most discreet, that he supposed he must get him a son by his Lady as duty did demand, though he himself but ill inclined and then he would be gone abroad for his enjoyment.

My dear I am weary of feasting and all the attendant discontent. Soon as the snow does ease shall I return to your sweet company.

'THE RARE, THE RIPE'

The same day that started off misty in Greenwich, dawned warm and sunny in West Sussex. Ardie pulled back the bedroom curtains and decided the day was a good one for going out.

Ardie had two overriding passions in his life: William Shakespeare and cars.

"Classic cars, you mean," he said grumpily to Frances when he overheard her describe them as old cars. "Not old cars. Classic cars."

At one time, thought Frances, she had been the passion of Ardie's life, with Shakespeare relegated to the working hours and cars kept as an interest for the odd spare moment. All other moments were dedicated to her.

Frances had a plan that one day she would buy Ardie a classic car of his own, for a very special occasion — their golden wedding perhaps or, since Ardie probably wouldn't regard that as special, in celebration of some amazing Shakespearian scoop that would stun the world. Since the arrival of Henry with his hints and his secrets, Frances had begun to hope that such an event might actually happen. To this end she was working obsessively on a book — a secret project designed to be a best seller, an overnight success, a money spinner. Ardie knew nothing of all this.

"Will you be alright, Henry?" she asked. "We thought we might go to an old car exhibition in Brighton. You're welcome to come if you want."

The young man had lived and worked under her roof for several weeks now and Frances would, on occasions, call him Henry. He never called her anything but Miss Goodbody. Seemingly deferential, he had a mocking look in his eyes that made her wary. He smiled up at her as he sat at Ardie's desk surrounded by mounds of paper.

"No thanks," he said. "Old cars bore me silly."

Frances nodded. "I know what you mean. As far as I'm concerned, cars either go or they don't. Usually the latter. I only have to get in the driver's seat and the wretched beast dies on me. Still, a car show's not too bad. You only have to admire the things, not drive them."

Henry ran his fingers through his dark hair rather wearily.

"It's not that. Kind of you to ask me but I've got too much work to do. Look at this lot!" He gestured towards the piles of papers. "These are all your husband's notes on Gilbert Shakespeare's journals. I'm glad you've made it your business to get involved yourself. Your notes are much easier to understand — clear, concise and to the point. But his — any day now he'll expect them to make sense!"

Frances shuddered. "I know. I'll have the nightmare of typing them up. Seriously though, Henry, you could give yourself a break. It is Sunday after all. I'm sure you're working too hard."

"Well," he said slowly, "got to be done. Time's too precious to waste."

Frances looked thoughtful. "The world's already wasted four hundred years not knowing the secret. Surely giving yourself a few hours off won't make much difference?"

Henry shook his head. "You don't understand. It's got to be soon. This year. They've got to know the truth." He stood up and walked over to the garden window, staring out blankly. When he turned round his eyes were very dark. "It's my life, Miss Goodbody. My one chance. My ancestor was Shakespeare. Think about it. The descendant of the great Shakespeare and no-one knows I even exist!"

Frances studied the young man. So that was it, in a nutshell. Nobody knew who he was. Henry Shakspeare, a bitter and frustrated young man with a twisted smile, needed to be known.

A couple of hours later Frances drove along Brighton sea front looking for a parking space. Ardie, for once in a genial mood, sat next to her. Frances, having resigned herself to dropping Ardie off outside the exhibition centre and driving two miles to find a space, spotted a car pulling out of a parking bay and swung in rapidly. The driver of the car in front of her, manoeuvering in order to reverse into the same spot, glared and hooted furiously but Frances didn't hear him. Her attention was diverted by a large brown seagull, twice the size of the others, that wheeled high above her head, screeching with triumph.

"Now listen, Frances," said Ardie in the Exhibition Centre, "I don't want you trailing round after me all day asking silly questions. Go and have a cup of tea or something. I'll let you know later what time I want to go back."

"Alright," said Frances mildly. Ardie strode off in the direction of the MGs, a purposeful look in his eye. Frances heaved a sigh of relief. They had got here safely, Ardie was in a good mood, the intricacies of the cars would give him plenty to think and talk about later. The day would be pleasant. She moved through the doorway into the main Hall.

The blaze of colour dazzled her. Five Cadillacs, red, green and pale-blue, on huge sheets of silver foil, sparkled and shone, their headlights gleaming and burning her eyes. One Cadillac reminded Frances of a bottle-green space ship. There it stood, aggressive and thrusting, its bonnet peeled back to display the complexity of its guts. Behind it, the display was in an early Sixties mode with a backcloth of red and white stars and stripes and a huge juke box blasting out rock and roll.

She wandered on, casually glancing at the exhibits.

"Oh look," cried a young woman, flapping her hand vaguely at the Daimlers, "Daddy had one of those."

Frances peered at a Daimler pedal car made in the 1930s and now the property of the Daimler and Lancaster Owners' Club. Perfect, miniature, child-size. DO NOT TOUCH it proclaimed in big letters. She wondered if a child had ever been able to touch, let alone pedal it.

Various small boys wandered past her, following doggedly in their fathers' footsteps and clutching dinky toy cars hastily purchased as a bribe for not being a bother. Frances noticed a few women hanging around, trailing wearily after their men folk. One was yawning openly, another tugged restlessly at her husband's sleeve, a third was chattering away brightly trying to look enthralled and intelligent. Several women were being supportive and manning the stands, ready, if the need arose, to answer technical questions. Quite a few were knitting.

Frances smiled to herself. It wasn't just the cars that were classic.

She wandered round as slowly as she could but had seen all she wanted in an hour. She spotted Ardie at one point, talking to a fellow enthusiast, looking animated and as if he would be there for ages. No point in trying to hurry him up, she thought, he'd only get more pig-headed than ever and refuse to leave until the bitter end. Besides, she liked seeing him absorbed and content.

She decided to amble round again slowly and have a good look at the displays, at all the props and people. Far more interesting than the cars, she thought. It struck her that many of the dummies and the models were dressed in 1930s style. It fitted in, was in keeping with the cars she supposed, but it was strange. Surely she herself had never worn a fur coat and a straw hat like the dummy on the Morris stand? Not together, anyway. As for all the imitation picnics, the parasols and the hampers and the pretend fruit, some of it was right, certainly — the spirit lamp, the soda siphon and the wind-up gramophone — but never the plastic thermos flask. Never.

She paused and studied a tin sandwich box that was part of another picnic scene. Did people really think that living in the Thirties was one long round of fun? The tin looked authentic enough, the sort of thing she remembered using in Cambridge on long, hot, lazy summer days by the Backs. In between the shadows of war. There were even real sandwiches in this box, noticed Frances, a nice touch, a careful touch — and she saw with amusement that one of the sandwiches had a large bite taken out of it. Of the stand holder there was no sign. Had he been overcome by pangs of hunger, she wondered — bored, restless enough to eat some of his own careful display — or had it all been intentional, the bite carefully taken, the moment frozen in time, the jolly picnic captured for ever on a camera lens? Frances hurried past. She didn't like moments frozen in time. It was best to keep moving.

Downstairs she followed signs to the Bargain Basement. All auto parts, lamps and levers and ancient car manuals. The man on the stand selling badges and car motifs looked more fed up than anyone Frances had ever seen. She contemplated buying Ardie a key ring but decided she didn't dare bother the man.

"Hello, Jim," shouted someone to him over the heads of the crowd. "How you doing?"

The man shrugged and glared at the mass of bodies surging round his stand. "Not too well," he muttered.

"You staying at a B & B?" called his cheery friend.

"Yeah," he said wearily, "some dump on the front. Got no sleep at all last night. Seagulls making such a racket."

"Welcome to stay with us tonight," said his friend, who Frances reckoned must be the original Good Samaritan.

"No thanks," said the other, looking more jaded than ever. "Probably sleep in the car park." He was determined to suffer.

Frances moved on. She paused and gazed at the Volvos for some time. The whole scene was set as a bridal scene, 1920s style, with the car decked out in ribbons. Frances stared at the dummy bride's face thoughtfully. She was gazing past the car, past the flowery bridesmaids, past her new husband, into some space in the middle distance. She looked wary. As if gazing down the years she had seen something that made her pause. Even the dummy groom had one fist clenched in his pale-blue suede gloves. France shuddered. What horrible ideas she gave herself.

She thought of Anne Cecil, who she had been reading about in the journals and letters, and of her wedding day that cold December long ago when, her heart thudding with excitement, she rode back in a coach from the Abbey ceremony to Cecil House; a child-bride to the handsomest young man in the land, dressed in a gown as white as the snow that fell, faster and faster, outside her carriage window.

"And all for what?" wondered Frances sadly. Anne Cecil, her father's pride and joy, his own Tannakin, married to a man who could never recall, from one day to the next, if it was his own wife he had slept with or someone else's.

"Oh there you are, Frances," said Ardie behind her, reassuringly near and normal.

She turned round and smiled at him. "Yes, love. Here I am."

"Have you seen the MG stand?" he said. She nodded. She had wondered if it would jog his memory at all. "Let's have another look, shall we?"

They strolled back across the now emptying hall to the stand which looked like someone's idea of The Great Gatsby or Brideshead Revisited. There it was, the MG 18/80 Mk1, exactly like the one Ardie had owned all those years ago, black and shiny with studs pinning down the soft-top, a klaxon at the front and running boards.

Frances rubbed her eyes. "Do you remember those running boards?"

Ardie chuckled. "I remember how I'd go driving off, thinking I'd said goodbye to you for the evening, and then you'd come charging down the road after me, jumping on to the boards. Clinging on for dear life. I never could shake you off. Always had to take you all the way back again."

"I never wanted to go," said Frances. "If I could hang on to you, I would."

"They were good days, weren't they?" said Ardie, gazing longingly at the car.

"They still are," said his wife.

Ardie turned and looked at her. "Are they?"

"Yes."

"Even though the best bits have gone?"

"Who says they've gone?"

"I thought they had."

"Then you were wrong, Ardie. As you usually are."

R. D. Davendish, old, learned and irritable studied his long-time wife.

"You know," he said, with something like affection, "I never could shake you off and bless me, I still can't."

EXTRACT FROM THE JOURNAL OF GILBERT SHAKESPEARE

SEPTEMBER 1574

The strange bright westward star that has illumined parts of heaven these two years now grows dim. I think it is a pale ghost doomed to fade unheard at cockcrow light.

Next month we repair to Hampton Court, my Lady Anne in much despair for the company of her lord. Pray God he may take observance of so fair a lady, begetting him the son he craves and bringing roses to the cheeks of her whose pallor and heaviness of spirit cause me much unease.

And so again we move, from house to great house, with no rest and always my poor lady in all her finery and silent tears.

This morning she did whisper to me in some distress concerning Oxford who has said he shall reduce her household for sake of good economy. What kind of man is this who lives to wild excess, whose extravagances are on every tongue, to act so mean towards so fair a Countess? In truth he loves the company of poets and of players and spends on them most freely, as he does in all the common stews, and yet his lady has to beg and weep before he'll pay her simple dues. She fears he'll cast me out and say I cost too much to keep in cloth and food and say I grow too old to be a tumbling boy, though small of stature still.

"I cannot let you go," she cries. "I will keep you as my page, my special serving boy, beseeching on my knees to keep you so."

"No, my lady," I cry in return. "I will not have you so distressed for my poor sake. I will stay with you though all the hounds of hell should try and force me out. I will clothe myself in rags and eat the scullery sops if needs must be but never shall I leave your side."

She smiled and wiped her eyes and said no need for such excess.

"All will be well at Hampton," says she. "This time I shall please him better."

She touched my face and my heart did leap and batter in its frame as though it would burst like the wildest stream.

Tannakin — for so I call you in my secret soul — would I could rid you of this cruel man who hates to see you smile. Were I your honoured lord, then hourly should I thank the heavens on my knees for granting me so rare a wife, so fair a jewel. But he — he tears the dreams from your dear heart and stamps them in the mire.

Though I be but a child and men mock at me, yet shall I serve you all my life.

JOURNAL OF THE EARL OF OXFORD

LONDON, JANUARY 1575

Tomorrow we depart and no man happier. Paris, Strasbourg, Venice, Florence, Rome — the very names cause my poor head to spin with giddiness and fear lest cruel fate shall at the last prevent my journey.

No. No need for fear. The Queen consents, my Lord Burghley too, though with much heavy muttering and tedious words of warning so that my brain did ache with boredom. My wife bids me farewell with trembling lip and tearful eye and I in haste to leave must play the patient husband still though my very soul screams out 'Go! Go! Go!'

In truth the world is mine. Farewell dull England, slumber still. I leave you to your stupor! My stallion stamps and whines; his breath is hot on my impatient hands and though the wind howls most fearfully, the rough sea draws me on. Never did Odysseus set sail with more hopeful heart than I.

God be with me now. May light of dawn break soon. I would be gone.

'DESPITE MY CARE'

Frances woke up in the grip of a dream. Outside it was still dark. She snuggled down under the covers next to the warm body of her husband and lay there, willing her dream to come back. She found she could do this quite easily as long as she didn't sit up or fidget around too much. They were all still there, the tatters of night, like the murky shapes of fish deep down in the river.

This time she was back in Cambridge again, running after Ardie's shiny, black MG down a long straight road and he, not seeing her, was getting up speed, accelerating away into the distance. Behind her, she realised, was Ellis, not moving, not doing anything, watching the car pull away.

Through the chinks in the curtain Frances could see early patches of light. She remembered the words of Emily Dickinson who forbade the 'yellow noise' of sunrise to disturb the dead in their churchyard graves. She enjoyed that idea. These days she seemed to be thinking about death and graveyards more and more. The effect of old age, she supposed. One no longer felt the immortality of youth.

Ardie grunted and muttered something in his sleep, tossing restlessly. Frances gently pulled the covers back over him. It seemed alright to her that they should be growing old together. Whether the best was yet to be was another matter.

She heard the first bird of the morning start up in the garden and imagined it perched in the cherry tree that practically shoved its pink blossom through her bedroom window in springtime. Soon other birds would begin their measure. She liked the idea that each one had its own time of beginning, like instruments in an orchestra or voices in a choir, ready and poised for their part.

Were they two branches of one tree, Ardie and herself, facing the setting sun together as the song said? She supposed this could be a description of their lives, of any couple's lives if they stayed together long enough; but it still didn't seem quite right for her and Ardie. They had started off strongly and solidly enough, no doubt of that, with mutual respect, admiration and affection, full of hopes and excitement in spite of a dangerous world. And there had been a child on the way ... But two branches? They had become so different, so divergent, still fastened to the original trunk, but hardly the same tree now.

She came to with a start. Had she been drifting off to sleep again? Her dreams were so real. Sometimes she found it hard to tell the difference between sleeping and waking. She felt a bit like Shelley who found himself 'absorbed like one within a dream who dreams that he is dreaming.' Frances loved quotations like this, enjoyed discovering and memorising them, copying any that seemed significant into her notebook. As for dreaming — night dreaming, day dreaming — she spent so much of her life doing that. Always had. Was that where all of the years had gone? Merged into dreams?

She slid carefully out of bed trying not to wake her husband. It was time to stop these foolish imaginings and get on. The early hours, while it was still quiet, were valuable to her. She could think, make notes, write her books, especially the new one which was filling all her thoughts with excitement at the moment. Pulling on her dressing gown she made her way downstairs, pausing in each room to open the curtains.

In a nearby garden she could see the neighbour's cockerel, strutting and preening himself in the early light. Some people objected to the bird, blaming it for waking them up too soon, but Frances liked it a lot. In an idle moment recently she had told Ardie he was her Chanticleer, like the cock in the fable. He had chosen to take this remark the wrong way, thinking she implied he was big-headed and boastful. In fact she had been thinking of the attractiveness of the bird 'of beautiful voice and feather' as Chaucer described him. Ardie had certainly been charismatic once — still was, in spite of his faults — her own Chanticleer who must be kept safe.

FROM THE EARL OF OXFORD TO SAMUEL HOWARD

FEBRUARY 1575

Sam, when will you come? Who else but you should share delights of this strange and brilliant world? I grow impatient for your converse soon. You sluggard, why so slow? Now make haste for Paris or for Venice where we must repair as soon as suns of early spring may thaw the mountain ice.

We have been here a month although the heaving seas did nearly wreck our hopes within a day of leaving England's shores. I tell you I did fear I was but food for fish. No matter, for the devil must protect his own and I did land with my poor retinue full sick and trembling but alive and with a hopeful heart.

The weather was most vile — the cold so biting raw my teeth did chatter all the while like a new fledged bridegroom at his wedding bed! The hours of day were as deep midnight and our horses stumbled in the rutted and most perilous roads, but hostelries there were in good abundance with wenches fair enough to thaw the blood and good mulled ale to ease our weary bones.

I think it fair to travel forth not knowing what adventures next. Oh Sam, would you were here!

For now we take our ease in Paris, an opulent and most bright realm with a multitude of men and sights to see. Some declare it is a seat of learning for great tongues and sciences but I would travel further on to taste Italian joys.

We are well received at Court with compliments and much expense. I shall whisper more in secret of the King with whom Dame Gossip gives herself much merriment since he does dote and take delight in young men mignons of the court who dress themselves in silks and furs as ladies of the night.

My creditors do murmur and would defurnish me in Paris but I needs must have provision for myself in these uncertain days.

The sun grows warm upon my back and men declare that spring will soon be here. My commendation to you. Pray God you travel swift.

Oxford

NOTES IN THE EARL OF OXFORD'S JOURNAL

MARCH 1575

Now must I write in fulsome terms to Cecil, give him thanks for sending me a messenger from England with news my wife is heavy with our child.

I will have my picture made and sent to her with gifts and wishes for her health and hopes the babe may prove to be a boy.

For if a boy then he will be a son to me and share my name and duties as a man.

But if they think to take occasion of this news of fatherhood to pull me back to England then my mind is very far from such opinion yet.

JOURNAL OF THE EARL OF OXFORD

ITALY, MAY 1575

And so against thick storms of snow and fighting for our very
lives, we crossed the Alps to Italy and thence to welcoming
sun that shines on buds of summer flowers.

Soon must we repair to Venice where men do say that if a
traveller should step into a gondola and give no sign where he
would go, the boatman takes him to the dwelling of a whore,
but such a whore as is protected by the state and clothed most
fair and her house as fine as that of any lady in the realm.
Would it were so in England.

JOURNAL OF THE EARL OF OXFORD

VENICE, SEPTEMBER 1575

Here we are made most welcome by the ambassador who offers us his residence until such time as we shall find or build a dwelling of our own. And I shall reside here many months for the life of Venice pleases me, and the company too. This is a shining, watery city full of light where tapers beckon me from every door.

Now must I send to Cecil and ask his favour for a loan of many crowns I borrowed for disbursement of my costs and beg that he shall sell for me some Cornish lands of mine.

News arrives from England though its passage long delayed. Now must I seem glad and write to Lord William and thank him for the news he sends to say my wife was safe delivered in July — a girl who they have named Elizabeth for the Queen.

JOURNAL OF THE EARL OF OXFORD

LOMBARDY, SEPTEMBER 1575

Sick and weary and fearful of the fever. Lombardy a furnace in this summer heat. Stench and flies are like a vision of hell.

Low in spirits and sick at those who would summon me to England binding my soul with duties and with debts. My Lord Burghley imagines now my wife has borne my child that I should hasten home and play the husband, but sweet Jesus could I leave all this for one whose face I scarce recall, who even now presents me with a daughter and no son. God forgive me for a sinner but I long to be away. Florence, Sicily, Rome, Greece — these are enchanted names that call to me like flares held high on dark and misty nights. My fever makes me rave. I would be well. God grant I never need return, never see those hated English shores.

'LEAVE ME IN MY CHURCH'

Frances, reading Oxford's accounts of his travels and all the other scraps of letters with their whiffs of rumour and gossip, became aware of the watchers in the shadows, the silent figures off stage. How surrounded Oxford was by Burghley's spies. In later years, as she knew, Sir Francis Walsingham developed the spy network to a fine art: training recruits, setting up agents, double-agents, counter-agents … he was the master of the underhand, peeling off the layers of secrecy like an onion skin, watching and waiting until the trap was ready to be sprung and then there would be terror in the night as men like wounded rabbits squealed in pain. Frances shuddered. She had read about the way conspirators were slaughtered — slowly, agonizingly and with sadistic relish, their heads on spikes like notches of success upon a stick.

But Burghley too, Anne's beloved father, he began it all: the secret spies, the undercover plotting in security's name, the deciphering of the codes. Frances smiled to herself as she thought about secret messages. Children down the ages had always loved cracking codes. She remembered writing letters herself in milk or lemon juice, warming the paper over a candle until faint writing showed. No wonder Burghley and Walsingham had so many recruits. It must have appeared to some as a very grown up game.

How hard it would have been though, working out the ciphers. It wasn't a matter of shuffling the alphabet or writing in lemon juice. Some codes could only be understood by placing a sheet of paper punched with holes over the top so that the relevant letters making up the message could be read. Success depended totally on calculating the exact sequence of thousands of holes. Almost as hard, thought Frances, as trying to break the Enigma Code at Bletchley during the war years, working for hours at a machine with variable elements, straining at scrambled, incoherent cipher-text.

But Oxford — Frances paused in her reading — to what extent was he affected by his father-in-law's network of spies? While Oxford was living in Venice, Lord Burghley made sure he knew every detail of the young man's way of life, from the sixteen year old choirboy Orazio Cogno, with whom the Earl was said to be enamoured, to the rich Venetian courtesan Virginia Padoana, whose company he loved to keep. Every coin that Oxford spent, every debt he ran up, soon found its way into Burghley's private notes. The Earl himself, with the help of his devious friend Rowland Yorke, fanned the flames of rumour and discord about his wife and baby daughter in England, but in the end, against the Burghley network, he didn't stand a chance.

It all went further back than that, thought Frances, reaching for her writing pad to make herself some notes, knowing that Ardie would very soon demand instant summaries from her of all the relevant people in Gilbert Shakespeare's life. Oxford had lived in Burghley's household for several years, been his ward-of-court and educated there, grown up with Anne in her childhood years, become betrothed and married to her ... and all the time Lord William's spies kept watch.

Frances pulled out her reference books to check the story of Thomas Brincknell, for this was the case that had the most damaging repercussions on Oxford's reputation. Thomas, so said the records, was an under-cook at Cecil House and while the seventeen year old Earl of Oxford and a tailor named Edward Baynam were practising their fencing moves, the said Thomas Brincknell ran upon the sword and was killed.

There was more to it than that, Frances was sure. Rumours were rife that Thomas was in the pay of Burghley and was spying on Oxford on his master's instructions. The hot-tempered young man, so went the story, spotted him lurking in the shadows and turned on him in rage, stabbing him in the groin so that he rapidly bled to death. Whatever the truth, Burghley covered it up, managed to fix it with the authorities so that it was recorded as a verdict of suicide. Thomas Brincknell, so said the account, had slain himself, deliberately and maliciously against the laws of God and the Queen, thereby disturbing the peace and dignity of the whole realm.

Frances felt her head throbbing with anger. Poor Thomas, accused of throwing himself upon the sword as a crazy way of killing himself. Because the verdict upon him was suicide, his body could not be buried in holy ground and his whole estate was forfeit to the crown. His widow Agnes and three year old son, Quyntyn, were forced into poverty, reliant on the parish for its charity or otherwise.

That afternoon Frances drove into Chichester. The next in her series of lectures on Victorian poets was due to be given in September and she needed to check out local connections with John Keats, the subject of her talk. As she drove she was still thinking about Burghley's spies, in particular the ones he positioned like small, squat shrubs in the households of his nearest and dearest. There were several, she knew, in the de Vere homes at Heddingham and Wivenhoe: quiet retainers who brushed Lady Anne's hair, rocked the cradle, brought candles and goblets of red wine to Oxford's unsteady hand — retainers who watched and reported. Burghley knew exactly how often, or how infrequently, his son-in-law visited his wife's bedchamber, how many times he threatened her with ugly words, how often he made her weep.

Not that Burghley needed spies in the household, thought Frances, pulling into the car park by the cattle market, for Anne told her father everything. She recalled a letter written by Anne, in the so-called 'reconciliation with her husband' later years, when the young woman, in the final days of her last pregnancy, had reported to her father how she wept all night, crying herself to sleep because of Oxford's temper and unkindness.

As she wandered down the street towards the Cross, Frances was still wondering about Anne Cecil de Vere. What sort of a woman was she? So little was really known about her. Gilbert Shakespeare adored her — and, so it seemed, with the sad exception of her husband, did everyone who met her. Several times Frances had come across the word 'sweet' used by Anne's contemporaries to describe her. Small of stature, gentle, docile and sweet. No wonder Oxford had been so restless, had champed at the bit. Not surprising he had fallen crazily in love with the notorious Anne Vavasour. There were two Annes in his life, the good girl and the bad. Is that why he went for the bad girl, she wondered, because his own sweet wife told tales?

"This won't do," muttered Frances to herself as she wandered round the outside of the old Cathedral, "you've come here for Keats, not the Shakespeare crew!" She shivered and shoved her cold hands into her coat pockets. Although the sky was a bright blue above the grey of St Richard's stone, there was definitely a chill of autumn in the early September air. Leaves in the Cathedral grounds were starting to change their colour, she noticed — smudges of yellow like finger prints over the green.

"Why do I never remember to bring useful things like gloves?" she asked herself. She'd brought her notebook and several pens for jotting down impressions of John Keats who had spent some days in Chichester and the surrounding area, working the beauty and magic of the place into his poems, but she had no gloves and no umbrella either for sudden rain. She sat down on an empty bench and pulled her notebook out of her bag, flexing her fingers to warm them up.

'Keats used the imagery of Chichester Cathedral and his impressions gained from attending a service at Stanstead Chapel, to create a medieval, gothic atmosphere for his poems on St Agnes Eve and The Eve of St Mark,' she wrote.

She sighed impatiently. No, that would never do. Didn't describe it at all, the imagination of that young man already sick with the illness that would kill him soon — the imagination that could visualise golden threads embroidered on dull brown cloth, or see the brilliant blaze of stained glass in a dirty-grey plain window.

It was no good. The ghost of Keats was as elusive today as the phantoms of the soon-to-be dead that he imagined in his poem.

It was thinking about Anne Cecil so much that had done it, made her introspective like this. A subservient, sweet woman — was that how people saw her, Frances Goodbody, a leading authority on Victorian poetry, valued for her research and lecture tours on the social life of Elizabethan England, a school governor, member of the parish council, the supportive wife of the author and scholar R. D. Davendish? She, Frances, one of the brightest lights of Cambridge in her day, an intellectual woman in a male-dominated society, adored and courted by the two most brilliant young men in the university circle ... subservient and sweet, was that what she had become? Was she really a classic case of 'the disappearing woman' subduing her own personality to that of her more extrovert and demanding partner?

Was it only now, when it was almost too late, that she was starting to reach out for something new and different, trying to smash the glass bubble, feeling the moth shaking its wings inside her, as Virginia Woolf had described?

She stood up abruptly, notebook and pens falling to the ground. She did not feel like a disappearing woman. Who was to say it was a mistake to spend one's life dreaming, to be absorbed in her dreams as she was? Keats wasn't the only one with imagination. She too had a mind that could seize on the slightest thing and make it magical and real. It was time to write to James, her literary agent and old friend of the family. Time to send him her brand-new manuscript that she'd been working on, obsessively, in secret. He'd probably be expecting some work of non-fiction about a Victorian poet. How surprised he would be when he found it was a novel. She couldn't wait for him to read it. It would be like starting over again.

It felt even colder now. Like Keats' chilly sunset she thought, gathering up her things. She decided not to go into the even colder Cathedral to see the poet's 'sculptured dead.' At this moment she didn't want to consider how they might 'ache in hoods and mail.' It was bad enough having a vivid imagination without encouraging it to delve into the gothic. Let the dead be sad and cold if they must. There was enough ache in her own life. She hurried away from the Cathedral grounds feeling that even the trees were watching her.

LETTER FROM AN ANONYMOUS OBSERVER TO A FRIEND

APRIL 1576

Here are strange, unnatural tales, spread abroad by fires of Rumour though I have been witness for myself to some of this.

Gossip says the Earl of Oxford, who has been on foreign soil these fifteen months, now makes sudden haste for England, wild of face and mien. They say he has a mind to quite cast off his wife the Countess, believing rumours that declare the daughter born to him last year is none of his and he is a cuckold like any common man.

They say he murmurs to himself 'I only lay with her at Hampton, no place else' and though some folk declare the child was delivered in July, others say it was September and Lord Burghley has made cover of the deed, which makes the space of eleven months and that too many moons even though it be a full term child.

I know not of the truth. Men say the Lady Anne is virtuous and falsely wronged and Oxford so much in his cups he would not know which whore he lay with nor even when or if it were his wife.

I fear there is much harm and whispered spite from those who would rejoice to see a breach between the families of Cecil and de Vere.

And some recall that Oxford never spoke of doubt until this time. They say, he had a portrait of himself brought into England for his wife to show his pleasure at the birth as well as two fine horses as a gift.

Now he does say he much mislikes the Cecil ties and would be glad by any means to free himself from those who hang, he says, like chains about his neck.

JOURNAL OF GILBERT SHAKESPEARE

APRIL 1576

And so my Lord Burghley and my Lady Anne in much distress of mind. Thomas Cecil did travel on ahead to Dover at my Lord's request to meet the Earl at his homecoming. My Lord William did advise his daughter not to go and greet her husband until she should understand his discontent, but she would not be satisfied to wait Lord Thomas's return and with Lord William, Lady Mary de Vere and my poor self went down to Gravesend where my Lord did write by several messengers to the Earl but received no answer.

Thomas Cecil then sent message that the Earl did land and leave the barge and took a wherry and straight to Rowland Yorke's dwelling, which news did grieve my Lady for men do say that Yorke is the harbinger of all these cruel tales.

Then my poor Lady did send messages to her husband with request that if he should not come that night to her father's house she would come to him, for she desired to be one of the first that might see him. Now he replied not, but sent message that there was a coach prepared for my Lady Mary his sister only to come to him, at which my Lady Anne did weep distractedly, requiring her father that she might go to him as well, but he said she should not go until the cause of the Earl's misliking were better known.

So all men troubled at these sad events. Would Rowland Yorke were here and others who have so poisoned Oxford's mind against his virtuous Lady, I would run him through a hundred times despite of my deformity and turn him on a spit like roasted boar until he squealed for mercy but none would I give. I fear so for my Lady.

LETTER (ANON)

APRIL 1576

In haste to tell you news that buzzes round our London town like a swarm of many bees for now the noble Earl of Oxford does disown his wife, incurring condemnation and the Queen's own wrath, but for this he seems to have no care.

They say his heart is turned by calumny quite against his lady now and he, unheeding of her reputation or the daughter he casts off, makes no provision for their care but says that they must live as charges in Lord Burghley's house and at his cost.

All men are divided. Some are glad to see the upstart Cecils brought so low while others grieve for their distress and curse the Earl of Oxford's name.

'A MIGHTY PULSE'

Henry Shakspeare walked out of Charing Cross station as the evening rush-hour crowds were beginning to move into it. He stood for a moment, trying to get his bearings and adjust to the noise of traffic and the urgency of people in a hurry.

He was glad to be off the train. The hypnotic effect of parks, gardens, allotments, and flats with their layers of windows and balconies empty except for occasional fuchsias or geraniums, had left him feeling a bit queasy and with a headache, as if one of his dreaded migraines was about to attack.

There was still a slight drizzle and signs of an earlier heavy rain in the damp forecourt of the station. Henry stared up, as he always did, at the Charing Cross monument, where a king had ordered a cross to be built at every halting place where his wife's funeral cortege rested on her final journey to the vault. Eleanor, the monarch's 'dear queen,' his 'chere reine.' Did he love her so much, wondered Henry, moving out into the Strand, or was it a formality? The expected thing for a king to do? He began edging his way towards the city's theatre land. Who was he to question what a man might do for love?

Reaching the Lyceum Theatre he paused. This was what he had come for, or at least been sent for, to observe and make notes about Cecil House and imagine what it might have been like in the days of Oxford and Anne.

"Soak up the atmosphere," Ardie had instructed. "Let's have a piece about stepping back in time to Tudor London. We're getting a lot of convincing stuff on Gilbert Shakespeare but better focus on Oxford for a bit. I must have all the facts and answers at my fingertips to show fools like Ellis that they've got the wrong man in Edward de Vere. I know we've got his letters but it's background we need; lots of background."

Henry shuddered. What an impossible task. Focus on Oxford with his bewildering, passionate, complex character, re-create a vast, stupendous, waterside mansion underneath and alongside London's theatre land? There were reference books in plenty: Ardie would do best to dig his information out of them or, more likely, get Frances to do so.

Henry stepped carefully away from the Lyceum and the queue that was beginning to trail down the street for the evening show. There had been several great palaces in this area — Somerset House, York House, Arundel House, the Savoy Palace — all rich and ornate with fabulous gardens and their own steps and river gates leading directly onto the Thames. Cecil House itself had stretched almost as far as Covent Garden in its heyday. Best to go in that direction and get a bite to eat at the same time.

As he walked, pausing to peer into brightly lit shop windows with their opulent displays of diamonds and furs, he tried to imagine the twelve year old Edward de Vere's journey to Cecil House. The young boy's father had died and there he was, the new Earl of Oxford, summoned out of Essex to be a ward of court to William Cecil, one of the wealthiest and most influential men in Queen Elizabeth's land. 'The boy in black' — that's how a London diarist had described him, with seven-score horse, also in black, and one hundred and forty men in mourning. The slow procession must have stretched for miles.

Henry found his way obstructed by a cluster of pigeons who were pecking hungrily at invisible crumbs on the pavement. One took off, right in front of him, zooming over the roof of a car which must have tipped the bird's wing because the pigeon fell under the wheels. Henry looked back to see what had happened to the bird, but there was only a bloody heap in the road and a few white feathers floating in the air.

Reaching Covent Garden, the smell of hot food reminded him how hungry he was. Thinking his queasy stomach wouldn't take to greasy onions or fried sausages, he settled for a cup of tea and chicken sandwich from a stall. A busker with an accordion was packing up in a corner of the street and a guitarist and a harmonica player with a wickerwork box full of mouth organs, moved into his place.

Covent Garden was as busy as it had been all day. A crowd gathered round a street artist who was creating a river scene on the pavement. Henry, eating his sandwich, joined them. The artist, working in chalk, coloured the boats that crowded the waterways, much as they would have done in Queen Elizabeth's day along the Thames by Cecil House and the other fine mansions. Such scenes of activity there must have been, with barges and wherries and the cries of London boatmen echoing down river: 'Eastward ho, Westward ho, Heave-ho, Rumbelow.' Henry could almost hear them. The artist started chalking in lights along his embankment: bright patterns of red, green and blue. Gilbert Shakespeare, peering out of an upstairs window, must have been aware of such a Venetian air every night time, with torches of fire, candles, gilded barges, white swans and the moon and stars like pieces of silver reflecting deep down in the water.

The buskers were into their Dylan songs now, the haunting tones of the harmonica underscoring the isolation of the tambourine man. Smoothly the melody glided through lament and protest. 'How many times must I go on doing this,' thought Henry, 'being a bystander.'

The artist must have become bored with his pretty river scene because he was now chalking out the lines of a tall gibbet on the bank, with a shape dangling from it and what looked like a raven hovering above. Henry moved closer and peered at the shape: a bundle of rags, it was timeless, could have been anywhere. In Tudor times, he knew, there were several riverside gibbets where the bodies of executed criminals and pirates were left to rot in their chains as a deterrent to others. The most notorious gibbet was near Rotherhithe, at a place named Cuckold's Point. He had never been there and had no intention of going. There were no connections there with Oxford or the Burghley lot.

He took a sharp breath. Of course there were links! The name Cuckold's Point derived from a post with a pair of horns on the top indicating a cuckold: a man whose wife had cheated on him. How the Elizabethans had loved their cuckold jokes, prancing about on the theatre boards with horns on their heads. Falstaff, bumbling around as Herne the Hunter in the forests of Windsor was a classic case. Henry had played the part of Falstaff himself when he was fresh out of drama school, on tour in the Midlands. He remembered stuffing yards of padding in his doublet to make himself look fat. The horns had been so awkward to wear. Gilbert Shakespeare knew exactly what he was doing when he wrote that scene. It was no joke.

Henry set off back down the Strand, walking briskly and thinking hard. Why should animal horns suggest betrayal and infidelity to the Elizabethans? Were those horns really meant to suggest the shape of the crescent moon, Lady Fortune herself, capricious and blind, the waxing and waning of love?

He decided to stop at a pub on the corner and have a beer. It was hot and stuffy inside, with a juke box pounding and people yelling above it. Henry took his drink and went outside into the front garden and sat at a picnic table. It was chilly in the September air and there was still a faint drizzle of rain, but at least it was quiet and he wouldn't feel obliged to make small talk with strangers at the bar. Who was he kidding, pretending to care about Oxford and his marriage problems, when he, Henry Shakspeare, the descendant of the world's most famous playwright, was a cuckold himself.

A girl passing through the garden glanced at the young man sitting on his own and paused, wondering whether he might be worth her time. Young women often noticed Henry, found him attractive in spite of, or because of, the birthmark across his face, but were usually put off by his cold, and frequently hostile, manner. Henry, if he noticed their attentions, considered possibilities and usually decided against them. Since Felicity he had allowed no woman to get close, to breach his defences.

He tipped the dregs of his beer over a bush and walked back into the Strand. Bruce Springsteen was belting out a song of freedom and escape from the jukebox and he could still hear its strains as he strode along.

'That's more like it,' he thought. 'My kind of music.' How he had identified with the song in his young rebel days, exhilarated by its savagery and madness. He remembered how he had played it over and over one evening, and Felicity had been there, loving and warm in his bed, and they had sung along with it, both of them, shouting out the refrain, happy for once and glad to be together, wild with the notion of dicing with death.

'WITH TOOTH AND NAIL'

"Sort this out for me, Frances," said Ardie, peering at his wife over the top of his spectacles as they sat at breakfast. "Henry won't want to be bothered and I haven't got the time myself. You sort it out." He tossed a letter across the table. "I daresay you know about it already."

Frances, finishing her toast, skimmed through the letter.

"Why should I know about it already, Ardie? You're the one they're asking for a paper on Provosts of King's. How on earth would I know anything about it?"

Her husband scrunched his spoon irritably through the shell of his boiled egg.

"Because of Ellis. I know about your secret letters, the sneaky little messages going to and fro. There's not much escapes me, you know. Not much I don't know about. Don't tell me he hasn't written to you all about this symposium. You must know he's presenting the main paper on M. R. James, though why they should think Ellis is any kind of an expert beats me! I'm sure I know far more about James than he does."

Frances stared at him blankly, wondering if paranoia had finally tipped her husband over the edge.

"No, I didn't know about it," she said. "Why do you always imagine Ellis tells me things?"

At the back of her mind images flickered briefly — a dark church on a misty evening, an inscription, a shadow, Ellis touching her … She sighed and the image fled.

"He'll enjoy that," she said calmly. "James always did appeal to his morbid fancy."

"Well," said Ardie, his eyes sparkling dangerously, "we'd better make sure that my paper's even better, hadn't we? Mind you, it's quite flattering really if you think about it, the fact that they've asked me to prepare a paper on one of the lesser known Provosts. After all, everyone's heard of James and read his ghost stories or seen them on some silly television programme, but I doubt if many people have heard of Dr John Argentine!" He gave a satisfied sniff and peered into his tea leaves. "Any more tea in the pot?" He pushed his cup across the table at her.

"Plenty," she said, passing the cup and teapot back to him. "Help yourself." She hesitated, wondering whether to display her ignorance. "I'm not sure I've heard of him myself, Ardie. This Dr Argentine I mean. When was he the Provost? Which century? I don't think I know anything about him."

Her husband looked at her pityingly.

"Oh late medieval or round about then," he said. "Richard III or Henry VII, that sort of era. Have a look round my library if you like. Bound to be lots of stuff on him. See if you can find out something a bit different. Make sure my paper's streets ahead of that prig Ellis." He rose to his feet looking satisfied, as if the fight was already won. "I'm going into town for a couple of hours," he called, as he headed out of the door. "Use my study while I'm out if you like, then you needn't worry about disturbing me."

He vanished, leaving his wife sitting among the breakfast dishes.

"I have got other things to do, you know!" she yelled at the slamming door. Slowly she counted up to ten.

Two hours later, Frances's neat little study was as chaotic as her husband's. In a gesture of defiance she had carted armfuls of books out of Ardie's shrine, dumping them all on her little table by the French windows. There she sat, with a sheaf of clean white paper, prepared to make pages and pages of notes. Now, with the noon sun creeping high in the sky, all she had found out about Dr John Argentine was that he was physician to Edward V, the youngest of the Princes in the Tower, and that he was later rewarded by Henry VII for various services by being made Provost of King's College, Cambridge. That was it. No new revelations to startle Ardie's audience into murmurs of appreciation, not even enough information to fill a single sheet of paper.

At this rate Ellis need do no more at the symposium than fix his compelling pale-blue eyes on the listeners, seeming to gaze into their very souls as he was so good at doing, before reading a few paragraphs of James' magnetic, terrifying prose. They would be his, eating out of his hand, their god for the day. Ardie's Roman nose would be well and truly out of joint and he would be unbearable to live with. Even more so than usual. Frances shuddered, cursing for the thousandth time the rivalry between the two of them.

"I'll have to invent something myself about this wretched Argentine man," she thought despairingly.

A shadow fell across the paper. Glancing up she saw Henry making his way furtively across the garden to the gate.

"Henry," she called through the half-open door, "come here a moment, will you?"

He walked slowly across the lawn, the look on his face very grim. "I was going to the post office," he said curtly. "Don't want to miss the collection."

"You won't," said Frances. "It doesn't go till one o' clock. I wondered, since you're going into town, if you'd call in the library and see if, by some miracle, they've got any information on this man who was Provost at King's way back. His name was Dr John Argentine and he was …"

"The last person to see the Princes in the Tower alive," said Henry.

Frances stared at him in disbelief. "The last person? However do you know that? I'd never even heard of him and nor had Ardie really."

Henry looked at her carefully. "I'm Shakespeare's descendant, Miss Goodbody. Obviously I've looked into the historical background to the plays, including Richard III." His tone softened. "I got to know quite a lot about it in my acting days, when I played the part of Hastings at the Aldwych. I'm sure Professor Davendish knows as much as I do. More probably. Must have forgotten. One of the drawbacks of old age, I guess."

Frances looked horrified. "Don't ever let him hear you say that! He'd never forgive us. Ardie prides himself on his phenomenal memory."

Henry smiled. "I'll look in the library for you." He turned to go.

"Hold on a minute, Henry," said Frances. "Help me get my thoughts straight, please. You said this man was the last person to see the Princes alive. How do you know that? You can't mean he murdered them!"

"Of course I don't mean he murdered them. No need to be so literal. I mean he was the last recorded person to see them alive before they were murdered. If they were murdered, that is. Before they vanished from sight would probably be more accurate. Dr Argentine was their doctor and he was called into the Tower to see the eldest one, Edward, who was pretty ill, suffering from toothache if I remember right. That's what showed up when they analysed his skeleton I think. If it was his skeleton."

"Toothache," echoed Frances. "Poor little boy." The sun had disappeared behind a cloud and a chill breeze ruffled the pages on her desk. "Fancy your skeleton showing you suffered from toothache!" She shivered. "Henry, thank you very much for this information. It gives me a few pointers to go on. I must be very ignorant. I thought I knew a lot of history but probably all I know about Richard III is Shakespeare's version and that's supposed to be cockeyed, isn't it? Tudor propaganda and all that. I mean, did he kill the Princes in the Tower or didn't he?"

"Oh, it's yet another one of the enigmas of history," said Henry, smiling at her.

Frances thought, not for the first time, how good looking he was when he relaxed.

"Almost as puzzling as who wrote Shakespeare." He laughed. "Don't go solving the Princes in the Tower mystery,

Miss Goodbody. It's the best whodunit ever and no-one will thank you. People love their mysteries."

"They certainly won't thank us for solving the identity of Shakespeare then. Providing the final answer."

Henry shrugged. "Probably won't believe us. However much proof we give them. We all believe what we want to. Don't want our little mysteries solved. Something to do with adding another dimension to our boring little lives. There's dozens of cases best left well alone."

"The Loch Ness Monster," said Frances promptly.

"Jack the Ripper."

"Amy Robsart."

"The Mary Celeste."

"The Bermuda Triangle."

"Back to the Princes in the Tower again!" said Henry.

"And Shakespeare," said Frances firmly. "The biggest puzzle of all. Who was Shakespeare?"

Henry paused as Frances fell silent. "Got to try though, haven't we? However much they'll hate us."

By three o'clock that afternoon Frances decided enough was enough.

'This is crazy, needing spectacles and a magnifying glass,' she thought as she rubbed her aching eyes and glared at the index where names and numbers danced and dazzled. 'All these books on Richard III and each one contradicting the rest!' She stood up slowly, willing the room to stop spinning, and pulled her long hair back into its untidy knot. 'Fresh air, that's what I need.' She gathered up her car keys, notepad and the last book remaining on the pile.

Some forty minutes later she decided to pull off the road, surprised to find she had been driving for so long with no clear idea of direction. Her head ached and she couldn't shake off a feeling of unease and foreboding. The sign post pointed to Bignor and Frances turned her green Datsun off the main road, crawling along the narrow, twisty roads that led to the Roman villa. 'I'll get some eggs on the way back,' she thought, passing a small cottage with large brown eggs for sale. She turned into the long drive leading to the ruins, hoping the cafe was still open.

Luck held. Frances, balancing a cup of coffee and a flapjack in one hand and her bag and book in another, made her way over to one of the low, wooden benches in the picnic area. She had visited Bignor many times before and knew the villa and its guide book almost by heart. Much nicer, she thought, to sit in the warmth of a mid-September sun with the soft, green hills of the South Downs all around her, white sheep grazing in the distance like toy farm animals and the smell of the rich brown earth. She felt her eyelids growing heavy and her tired bones relaxing in the sun.

'I could reach out my hand,' she thought, 'and touch a Roman farmer on the shoulder'.

"Look, do you want a drink or not?" said an impatient voice by her ear.

"No thank you. It might make me fat."

"Now you're being ridiculous! I never said you were fat. I said you're not as thin as you used to be but that doesn't mean you're fat!"

Frances sighed and opened her eyes. The angry couple moved away, still arguing. She watched as the woman squeezed herself into the passenger seat and slammed the car door.

Frances winced. 'Fancy coming here to have a row,' she thought.

She sipped her coffee which was growing cold. A young girl with short, red hair and long green earrings wandered over and flopped on the grass nearby, clicking on a transistor radio as she did so.

'No rest for the wicked,' thought Frances, licking the last of the sticky flapjack off her fingers and resignedly opening her book. Scraps of conversation came floating over from the ruins as she tried to concentrate.

"This corridor was originally thirty-one feet long. Can you imagine it?"

"Mmm. Long wasn't it."

"Lots of baths those Romans had."

"Yeah. Must've needed loads of towels."

"I saw a programme about the Romans on T.V."

"Was it good?"

"Not bad."

Frances stuffed her fingers in her ears and tried to focus on the print in front of her. The biographer of Richard III, who didn't seem to know a great deal about his man or have any new theories, had decided to give regular medieval weather reports instead.

'Palm Sunday 1461 was the Battle of Towton. A day of winds and heavy snow which turned to a blizzard blinding the men as they charged downhill against a storm of arrows.'

She turned over the page and wished she hadn't.

'By nightfall,' wrote the biographer warming to his subject, 'six miles of snow-covered ground was scarlet with the blood of twenty-eight-thousand dead and dying men. Not a single nobleman survived the carnage; all were beheaded on the spot. It was another Easter, a decade later, when the Battle of Barnet took place. It was still half-dark on a morning of fog and rain and in the dull and murky light the Lancastrians thought the livery of the Star with Streamers was the Yorkist Sun in Splendour and fired arrows at their own men.'

It all sounded horribly familiar.

'As if there's not enough killing in the world without firing at your own men,' thought Frances. The more she read of history, the more she reckoned mankind learned nothing.

This is how Cassandra must have felt, she decided, having the gift of prophecy but no powers of persuasion. A bit like me. Surely after all these years I should be wise enough to know how to change the whole rotten situation.

She put the reference book away in her bag. How long ago it seemed, those heady, fragrant days at Cambridge when they were all so young and full of hope. How had they got so petty? Was it old age? Where had that young girl gone with the world at her feet and the two cleverest, most handsome young men in Cambridge as her lovers? She could still remember. Not only remember but write it all down, most vividly, as she had been doing lately on lonely evenings. She sighed. What was the point of dreaming? Those days could never come again. It had all narrowed down to two old men screwed up with envy and rage and herself in the middle, dry as dust.

She knew what Shakespeare meant when he wrote 'And there is nothing left remarkable under the visiting moon.'

She was tired of trying to dig up the past. Surely she had got enough now on this Dr Argentine. That was what had done it, cast her in this melancholy frame of mind, all that talk about bones. What if the skeleton of the little boy did show he had toothache? The urn had also contained a large variety of animal bones. The building had been a zoo as well as a palace. What did it really matter whose bones they were for all that Shakespeare wrote cryptic verses cursing any disturbers of his.

She pulled her notebook towards her, re-read the last part of her notes. Dr Argentine had said the little boy king, believing he was facing a sudden and violent death, prepared for it like a sacrificial victim, seeking remission of all his sins through hours of confession and penance. She snapped the book shut. How ridiculous. What terrible sins could a little boy like that have committed? Why the need for such atonement? He must have had a death wish.

It was late in the day and she'd achieved very little. She'd better go and buy some fresh brown eggs for Ardie and maybe a bunch of flowers as well. Not that he would notice.

DYING BY DEGREES

Of course, it hadn't always been like that. Two bigoted old men sniping away at each other across the years, crowing and screeching like demented cocks at each petty triumph, each bull's eye scored bang on the other's ego.

Both boys had been born in the same year, in the same village, with the proverbial silver spoon in their mouths. Both wheeled around in smart perambulators by nannies or doting older sisters, their infant slumbers disturbed by nothing more strenuous than the sound of cricket bats on hard balls or the tinkling of fine china as the ladies sipped tea at croquet.

The first eight years passed smoothly, flowing as gently as the stream where the two boys fished for sticklebacks. No murmurings of war, no blood, no muddy death disturbed their games as they built camps, watching and waiting like secret agents for the passing enemy, leaving code messages in tree trunks, guarding it all like soldiers to the end. The few widows and mothers who sat muffling their sobs in the back pews of the church, the white stone monument erected in the village square with the names of honour carefully carved, the stained glass window in the grey Norman church with its flock of angels in red and blue donated as a memorial to the brave sons of the parish — all these things entered into the subconscious of the two boys and lay there.

When they were eight they were sent away to boarding school and if they sobbed at night grieving for home, hiding their tears in wet pillows, then nobody knew anything about it, nobody could tell in the morning. Maybe it was in those days that Timothy first learned to be secretive, to confide in no one, to bottle it all up, while Rupert became even more outgoing, ever busy, surrounded by friends.

And so they grew up, these two friends, Rupert, fair and strong, so easy going and attractive to be with and Timothy so dark but with those pale blue eyes that hooked people with their intensity, whenever he looked anyone full in the face, which wasn't often. An inscrutable boy, they said, that Timothy Ellis with his slightly hunched shoulders and an air of being watchful.

Clever boys with a flair for learning and a delight in literature and classics, they both went to Eton and later, with scholarships, to Cambridge, secure in their expectation of a brilliant future and united in a friendship that was strong, bold and brave, lasting to death and beyond. After all, had they not made a most solemn pact some time ago, in a darkened room lit by flickering candles, with blood pricked from wrist and finger and sealed in a firm hand clasp? Nothing could go wrong. So what did? Why, more than half a century later, were they so locked in this implacable hatred, this ludicrous war of nerves, this energy force that kept them both alive in the hope of seeing the other one dead?

Consider some moments frozen in time, a chink in the curtain through which images flicker.

The year is 1935. Ardie and Ellis, as now they call themselves, have both achieved brilliant degrees, Ellis by sheer hard work and nervous energy and Ardie by a natural flair for plucking learning from the clouds and a combination of luck and charm which others envy. Both are postgraduates aiming high — a coveted Chair of English at Cambridge is a distant but a heady goal. Research and original thought become goals in themselves and the list of articles, pamphlets and small publications is steadily growing. Ellis has the name for painstaking, logical thought whereas Ardie is known to take risks and to delight in producing shocking and surprising theories, but both are highly regarded. This year they are neck and neck, both breathing fast and furiously as, with bloodshot eyes and flaring nostrils, they pound towards the post.

In 1935 they are both fine young men. Ardie draws all eyes with his colourful style of dressing — orange neck-scarf tucked casually into a bright-pink shirt, a straw hat tipped over one eye, sunglasses worn in winter — the cantankerous old man who will only wear brown or grey and will foot the same pair of shoes for twelve years is far off down the future. At twenty-five Ardie is flamboyant and rejoices in the fact. He is rarely to be seen without an admiring crowd of acolytes who laugh at his jokes and drink his champagne and applaud every opinion, the more outrageous the better. This crowd always includes women — young students newly up, learned dons, mature society ladies, models, singers, actresses — all are glamorous, all are amusing and all adore Ardie. He could have his pick of any of them and, judging by a rather scandalous reputation which he cultivates, he probably does.

Ellis, on the other hand, is rarely seen with a woman. His desire for privacy, begun in the early years, has now reached exaggerated proportions. He has few friends, shares no confidences and if, on a dark winter's afternoon, he takes a woman to his single bed in his shabby Cambridge room, then no-one is any the wiser. Many a young girl gazes admiringly at his long, lean body and catches her breath at the burning intensity in his pale blue eyes, but of this he seems unaware.

Be that as it may, Ardie and Ellis are still firm friends. The bond is as yet unbroken.

It is at a cocktail party one November evening in Cambridge that Frances Goodbody enters the story: eighteen years old, blonde hair in a neat bob, simply dressed in a soft frock — there she is in that Cambridge room, taking her place with the cream of brains and beauty and there, amazingly, is Ellis, her escort for the occasion, unwillingly doing his social duty.

In 1935 young women do not go freely to cocktail parties, unchaperoned, but Frances feels she has the right to some independence. Besides, the hostess of the party is a distant cousin and she has invited Frances, cleared it with the Warden of the Student Hall and suggested Ellis should escort Frances.

"It won't kill you, Ellis," she said. "You've never been to one of my cocktail parties. You owe it to me. Ardie will be there later. Frances is a dear little thing. A bit timid and still a schoolgirl really, but quite bright. You won't be bored and she certainly won't eat you."

So Ellis dutifully does as he is told, collects the young lady from the Students' Hall and, apart from the fact that he tells her his boyhood name was Timmy, which she promptly takes as permission to use, he finds her charming. Certainly not boring as he had feared. As he looks into her clear, grey eyes, he feels an interest, a desire to know her more.

But now along the street, like sunshine on a dull November day, comes Ardie Davendish and a crowd of friends, prepared to be happy, willing to enjoy and be entertained, open to whatever life offers in this sparkling world. He pauses, his hand on the door knocker, ready to demand entrance to the party for he knows they are all waiting for him, anticipating him with pleasure like bubbles in cool champagne.

In Cambridge streets there are still lights hanging from the trees and coloured ribbons decking doors, for this is Jubilee Year.

Rarely had the weather been so fine as that week in May when Frances explored the city that was to be the centre of her life. "Long Live King George and Queen Mary!" cried the crowd, intoxicated on festivity and pageantry as they sang and danced in streets rich with bunting and Mussolini and Hitler were but shadows.

Frances had entered Cambridge on this wave of optimism, into this most ancient of cities where Rupert Brooke and bright young girls in straw hats had once gone punting down the river on lazy days and lain in fields at Grantchester, diving in the weir at Chaucer's Trompyntoune.

On this evening in 1935, she feels drunk, not on alcohol, for life is stimulant enough for her, but on the imagery and symbolism of her city of bells where heraldic beasts, Tudor Roses, angels, crowns and Fleur-de-Lys fill her soul.

Into the party comes the one person who can complete the enchantment. He notices her at once of course, for although the room is full of sparkling women, talking and

95

laughing and sipping their cocktails, fixing him with the full beam of their personalities, there is something about this young girl with her grey eyes and air of serenity that draws him like a magnet. Not that he shows it, for Ardie knows the tricks and plays the game too well to give it away, and although he knows she has seen him, he makes no move in her direction, keeping her only in the corner of his vision until the crowd has thinned and there is space.

Or is it Ellis that he notices? His best, his oldest friend. Does he notice, as an animal scents prey, that Ellis is unusually moved by this young girl, that for once he is letting his mask drop, that Ellis is enthralled? Does Ardie realise, as he walks slowly across the room towards the pair on the settee, how vulnerable his friend has become?

Is that where the twist of envy begins, the almost unconscious urge to take this girl off his friend, to spoil it, to come between, to assert himself as cock of the dung heap? Is this the first move in a bitter game?

"Good evening, Ellis," he says, looking steadily at the girl, smiling at her. "Who's this you're keeping to yourself? Aren't you going to introduce me?"

"Good evening, Ardie," says Ellis slowly. "May I introduce you to Miss Goodbody."

Ardie looks carefully at the two of them. Smiles again.

"Do you mind if I join you?" he says to the girl.

She looks at him, makes room for him next to her on the settee.

"Please do," she says softly. She is enchanted.

So was that the cause then? A conflict as old as the hills, a triangle, a sexual thralldom that was to bring them more grief than joy. Was that all it was, two men fighting over a woman and nearly tearing her apart in the process?

Surely there was more to it than that. These were two brilliant academic men, not dogs fighting over a bitch on heat. These were Shakespearian scholars, the brains of the country who debated and argued and wrote and supposedly understood all the conflicts that rocked the thirties and ripped the illusionist's tent wide open. Surely there were massive, worldwide issues that later wrecked the friendship of Ardie and Ellis as they argued fiercely into the long, long nights, disagreeing violently and hurling insults with all the vitriol at their command, for these were clever men, literary figures and good at word games.

Or was it all later on? Was all this the dynamite lit by a fuse the day that Ardie achieved his goal of Professorship at Cambridge and Ellis didn't, or when Ardie published his first major work on Shakespeare and Ellis counter blasted with such scathing denunciation of the theory that he won himself wide acclaim from the media and never looked back.

Or did it all begin a very long time ago in the woodland camp of two little boys playing soldiers?

"Bang Bang. You're dead."

"No I'm not!"

"Yes you are. I shot you!"

"You didn't. You missed."

"No I didn't!"

"Yes you did! I'm not dead yet!"

'SO FAIR SHE WAS'

Frances picked up a pebble. "Can you see a face in it, James?" She stroked the sand out of its grooves.

Her agent, who was admiring the sailing boats dipping and skimming like butterflies on the haze of the horizon, glanced down.

"It's a clown, a bit misshapen but still a clown. Look — there's his cap. There you go, Frances, it's laughing at us. Two silly people who can't get their act together."

He leaned uncomfortably against the wall, peering at the pier on which were a group of Birdmen in fancy dress attempting to fly. The beach, covered at the best of times with seaweed and debris, was packed with bodies as far as the eye could see. James shuddered.

Frances squeezed her hand round the pebble. "I don't think it's a clown. It's not laughing you know, it's screaming. Its eyes are hollow and its bones are swollen. It's a gaping death's head." She dropped the pebble into her handbag, clipping the clasp shut. "Scorched to a cinder one sunny afternoon when they dropped napalm on it. Probably a day like today." She smiled at her agent who pulled a face.

"Don't say things like that. Throw it away. For God's sake throw the horrid thing away."

She pulled her handbag more firmly to her. "No. It's my mascot. Bring me luck with my book. At least it's got a shape, a form. It has survived, James, it has survived."

She laughed at the sight of Colonel Sanders and his chicken staggering up the ramp, closely followed by a green octopus. "Look at them. Aren't they great? Don't you think they're wonderful?"

Her agent nodded grimly. "They haven't got a hope in hell of flying."

"Oh that doesn't matter. At least they're having a go. Isn't it a strange thing, James, the power of words. Just now when you looked at my pebble you saw a clown, the mask of comedy, didn't you? And now, with a few careless words, I've put a fresh image in your head and you're stuck with it."

"You're clever with words, Frances. Much better than me. That's why we're in this mess now, with that wretched book of yours. I can't keep up with you."

"It's not that," she said as the crowd swayed and cheered the Birdmen. "Anyone can do that with words — change an image I mean or fix something in someone's head for all time. Like a few years ago, someone told me that at this road near us, at the junction, there was an accident. Two poor lads on motor bikes — a head on collision. This person said, quite casually, that the two bodies went flying up into the air. Do you know, I can never drive past that junction, even in the middle of the day, without seeing those bodies flying up in the air. That's what I mean about how easy it is to plant an image."

"They've done it!" boomed the commentator, "I think they're the furthest so far! Colonel Sanders and his Chicken — Oh dear, the Chicken's head's come off. What a fowl thing to happen!"

"Oh let's get out of here," said James impatiently. "I'm too old for this sort of thing, Frances, even if you're not. My shoes are getting ruined."

"Serve you right for wearing such silly clothes. Fancy turning up in a suit. This is Bognor beach, not a Board meeting, you know. Why don't you make the most of this sudden burst of late summer? Everyone else is."

Her agent glared at her as they made their way through the crowds and stumbled off the pebbles.

"For a start, I didn't know I was coming to the beach. I thought we were going to have a nice meeting in a quiet, little restaurant somewhere and discuss bits and pieces. Why have you changed plans? It's not like you to go changing things. This is like something out of a nightmare." They pushed their way through the barrier of bodies and onto the pavement. "It all smells diabolical!" He mopped his brow.

"Oh I don't know," said Frances, as they squeezed their way down the promenade. "It's not so bad. Salt, sea and vinegar. What more can you ask for?"

"Anything but this!"

They came to a stop outside the Bognor Rocke Shoppe.

"Oh look," said Frances, "they sell thirty different flavours of rock. I've a good mind to buy them all and see if I can tell the difference."

"Frances Goodbody," said her agent, putting his arm round her, "you are impossible. If it wasn't for the fact that you are one of my oldest friends and I love you dearly, I would shake you until your teeth rattle for bringing me to this hell hole. How Ardie puts up with you, I will never know."

"And he will never know, because he doesn't really know me. So there's no problem, James."

Her agent looked at her thoughtfully. On the beach the crowd was screaming and waving wildly as Eddie the Eagle prepared to ski down the pier with rockets on his heels.

"The problem is this ludicrous book — a beautiful book I'll grant you: a pearl among books, elegantly written, sparkling and brave. But a ludicrous book for one of your reputation. Frances, please believe me. There's no way, as your agent, that I can allow you to market an erotic book."

Frances blew her nose angrily. Outside the amusement arcade a metal zebra rocked rhythmically as children clambered aboard.

"For a literary agent," she said scornfully, "you have strange ideas. We're not living in the days of Lady Chatterley you know. Books like mine are on every bookstall these days. There's no harm in it. You said yourself it's well written."

"Literary merit has always been a poor excuse for bad taste. Are you listening to me, Frances? Leave that stupid zebra alone!"

She sighed, slipping a final coin in the slot. "He likes rocking. He gets bored standing still with nothing to do. Like me," she added defiantly, moving away.

"You've got lots to do, Frances," said James impatiently, hurrying past the Kebab Palace. "All your articles on Browning — it's high time you sorted them out into another book form — to say nothing of all the research you do for Ardie. He may not admit it but I know how many hours you spend checking facts and correcting proofs. He should acknowledge your help more."

Frances stopped and gazed up at the Carlton Hotel.

"Looks pretty sick doesn't it? Sick and green. Like an old man with a gammy leg and a few stumps of teeth. One day it won't be there anymore. I'm bored with Browning," she said, turning to face her agent and blocking him in against the railings. "I'm bored with Shakespeare too, though you probably think that's heresy. Ardie doesn't need me all that much. He's got a new project and a new assistant and he's hell bent for the big scoop. So that leaves me. I've written a book for fun. An erotic book to see if I could do it, break out of the mould I've been stuck in for years and I have! It's as good as any other of its type and you know you could sell it, James — make it a best seller, a T.V Soap — the possibilities are endless. I want to be famous, for a few days or whatever. I want the fun of seeing my book on sale, with my name on it in big letters and my picture on the back cover — What's the matter, James? Why are you looking at me like that?"

She stared angrily at her agent who was wiping his brow and looking agitated.

"I'll give it to you straight," he said, speaking fast. "I could place this book, no trouble, probably sell the T.V rights as you say. If it was anyone but you I'd probably be jumping for joy at the chance of a best seller. But it's not you — I hate it for you — the image is all wrong." He stopped and mopped his brow again. "I'll do it on one condition."

In the distance they could hear the Radio Fun Bus with the presenter rousing the crowd.

"What condition, James?"

He took a deep breath. "That you don't use your own name. And that under no circumstances do you allow any interviews or T.V appearances. I'll handle all that side of it."

"Why, James?" said Frances, "I'm not ashamed of my name. It's the one I was born with. I'd have thought Goodbody was an excellent name for an author of a book like mine. Everyone will think I've made it up!"

"You can't write under your own name, Frances. Think what it'll do to Ardie! He'll be so ashamed and everyone will tease him cruelly about where you got all the erotic bits from. They'll say, 'You must be the husband.' He'll never live it down. I know you've got a vivid imagination, Frances, but other people will think it's based on real life."

Frances laughed. "Do you know the story about Harold Robbins, James? When some interviewer congratulated him on having such a vivid imagination and writing all those scandalous bits in The Carpetbaggers? The story goes that he looked at the interviewer with absolute contempt and said, 'Imagination? You haven't lived, mate!'"

James looked embarrassed. "Don't talk like that. I know you're trying to shock me and get your own back, but if you're telling me that all those bits in your book are firsthand experience, I don't believe it."

She shrugged her shoulders. "I was young once. Ardie might remember, though I doubt it. You could ask him. If he doesn't remember, then Ellis should." She looked thoughtful. "Yes, Ellis will remember."

"Well," said James, trying to move past. "You said it, not me. You were young once."

"Isn't an old woman allowed to write this sort of book? You think I'm old and past it and should know better? Why are you so bothered about Ardie? Whose side are you on here? Obviously not mine! You think it's disgusting, don't you. That's the truth of it."

"It's not that," said her agent. "Older women do write love stories and … and … books like yours sometimes. I don't think it's right for you."

"I see. Goodbye then."

"Where are you going, Frances?"

"Going? First of all I'm going to join that lot round the Fun Bus. Can you hear them clapping and chanting 'I'd rather be in Bognor than Hawaii?' So would I because it's real to me. It's here and now and full of life and fun and I want to be part of it. I've spent too much of my life living among dead writers. Time's 'winged chariot' is racing along and I've got things I want to do before it catches up with me. Then I'm going to have a bag of greasy chips smothered with vinegar and then — then I'm going home to write a few letters and see if there's anyone out there who'd like to act as an agent for an old woman."

"Oh Frances, why?" James looked distraught. "I only want the best for you, surely you must know that. You haven't listened to a word I've said."

"Oh but I have," she said, moving away in the direction of the Fun Bus. "I've listened to every word, including the ones you haven't said, and I despise every syllable of them. You and your kind have got a fixed and rigid image of me and you're determined I'll live up to it. I shall get that book published, in my own name, with my picture plastered all over it!"

"You'll see!" he shouted after her. "You'll ruin your reputation for ever!"

She yelled something back. The wind carried her words away but from the expression on her face he guessed it was rude. He saw her nearly trip over a large cardboard box that was blowing down the street and watched as she kicked it angrily away. FRAGILE. HANDLE WITH CARE it said. Frances walked rapidly in the direction of the Fun Bus.

LETTER FROM WILLIAM CECIL TO HIS WIFE MILDRED

MARCH 1581

My dear wife,

It grieves me deeply to write to you with news I know will cause you much distress of mind without the comfort of my own company, but think it wise to stay attendant on Her Majesty here at Kenilworth, and that way perchance may soothe the grievous harm lately afflicting our family by our most accursed son in law. Would I had never seen fit to rear him as my own, granting him much honour as a royal ward in my household, taking pity on a fatherless child for that the name of de Vere did signify much wealth and high rank. Most bitterly do I repent the joining of our noble houses, granting him the hand of our daughter when Philip Sidney was most ardent for her, though I thought his estate not so grand as Oxford's at that time. Now are we all in debt through his extravagances and the name of Cecil dragged down through his disgrace, giving my enemies much cause for rejoicing, while my poor girl, abandoned and scorned by him these five years since his return from journeying abroad at much expense to me, must now face attack and calumny again, so ill deserved, though the name of Cecil must protect her from the scorn of ignorant men.

Know then the news wherof Rumour spoke for once in truth, that Mistress Anne Vavasour, having been with child these last months by Oxford's doing, was delivered of a boy and the same night taken to the Tower at her Majesty's command and there locked up, as strumpets do deserve, with her bastard and I do much rejoice at such good news as will you, but word is spread abroad for Oxford's arrest also, though I did intercede with Her Majesty for our name's sake but she was in great fury and would not be changed. Some say he flies the country, but though his faults are many I think him not a coward and so expect to hear of his present capture, though he may not live to suffer his deserved affliction, for the drab's family do vow vengeance and her brothers have intent to make quarrel with him and so run him through, and if I heard he was dead in such a way I fear my heart would rejoice for the harm he does us all.

So now prepare our daughter that her lord will soon be within the Tower for getting the drab with child, which news I think will cause her much dismay for she would even now have him within her arms, for she is ever gentle and forgiving.

For myself I fear there may be danger, for my enemies surround me and I trust no man and though Her Majesty is ever gracious to our family, holding us in high regard for the love and duty we bear her, yet there are some who daily breathe a poison in her ear and would turn this our present misfortune to their advantage, rejoicing to see me brought down. Yet I am as one who fears no danger, having lived through times when a man might fall asleep, placing his allegiance where it seemed most safe and wake to find his head demanded as a feast for carrion crows.

Men at court do talk of our houses with wonder, praising always our gardens for their terraces and avenues and fountains and many fine and rare plants and Her Majesty does often say of all great houses in the land ours are of the finest. I think it fit to make preparation so she may honour our house at any time and none of us be thrown into confusion. And I think to send some costly gifts, a ewer of rock crystal perhaps, mounted in silver gilt, and some maps like those she much admires in our library at Theobalds with painted savages and turbaned Turks and gilded galleons and spouting whales that make her laugh and Tritons blowing horns, and I will have a portrait made of Gloriana standing on the world triumphant, then will men wonder and be amazed and show much honour to the name of Cecil.

Dear wife be not cast down by these sad events for always the tide does turn and the Queen may yet show Oxford mercy though he deserves it not, restoring him to favour for my sake. Now urge our daughter that she should write forgiveness to the Earl, not blaming him for the strumpet Vavasour nor yet bemoaning her poor state, for if they should be reconciled I think the Queen would be the better pleased and sooner show her favour once again, and though Oxford would much mislike it yet need they live as one in name only and not give rise to gossip, for five years is unseemly long to live apart and drabs like the Vavasour think to take advantage and scorn the name of Cecil.

So urge our daughter to be of good cheer and cease her grief, for I much mislike to see her wandering around like one lost in Hades with none for company save that poor boy she did take in as tumbler many years since. And though he much deserves our pity, I think he soon becomes a man and 'tis not fit my Tannakin should have but him for company although I know she dotes on him and he is a faithful servant. The years go past and she needs must breed a son with Oxford's name, though how such things can come to pass when he begets boy bastards but shuns the company of his fair wife I know not, nor understand his cruelty to her who I think most surely the loveliest of women, though she be my daughter and my opinion swayed.

Pray God our fortunes change before the year be out. Pray give commands for sending the Queen a chain of pearls and sapphire, finely made as showing our devotion, and I will presently oversee the handling of the other gifts on my return. Bid Tannakin remember, as I know she will, the name of Cecil still is one to hold with pride and she must not be cast down by her lord's misdeeds, the devil take him.

JOURNAL OF GILBERT SHAKESPEARE

JUNE 1581

My Lady in good spirits at the news of Oxford being released from the Tower and hopeful of his company by Christmas time, many letters passing between them wherein he begs forgiveness for wronging her so grievously these several years and vowing reformation; a sinner turned a saint, a veritable Augustine, but I do not believe him nor does the world.

The Feast of good St John comes near and my Lady begs her father bring some players in to give her cheer and fortitude at this most hopeful time. These players shall perform a foolish scribbling from my pen though none shall ever know the fountain whence it springs. I have in mind a tale of magic with nymphs or fairies small as cowslips, tiny as an agate stone, though none shall see them with the eye but as it were a dream. My lady loves good rhyme and all harmonious melodies so there shall be sweet songs and rondels that shall conjure her a garden bright with herbs and flowers of violets, oxlips, musk rose buds and eglantine and these fays must dance with bees and ride on wings of bats.

Yet there must be one who will prance and make a merry jest or else a shrewd and knavish pouke, a lob of spirit who will make my lady tremble though it be but for a moment for such shadows are but dreams and I would have them gone.

A bower of dreams be thine tonight
And sweet forgettings thy own guest
So may the goblin and foul sprite
Constrain'd be in vipers nests

JOURNAL OF GILBERT SHAKESPEARE

JANUARY 1582

A merry house or seeming so this past month with the Earl returned home though melancholy and with a frown, and my Tannakin in fine new robes and with a smile set always on her face as one fixed there as if she dares not let it fade. So much festivity and Lord William in a cheerful mood for Oxford now restored to favour with the Queen for playing at the dutiful husband once more, though my own heart is like a stone within my breast and I fear it cannot last for how can Oxford change? Yet did I turn my pen to use and make many scribblings for the players to act in celebration of twelfth night and many poems which the Masquers set to music, my Lord William allowing plays and songs in celebration of our new good hopes. My Lady whispers to me that Oxford has made promise that they too shall have musicians and a company of players at Heddingham, which pleases her for she intends my foolish works to be performed though my name be hidden as a bee within a flower.

And thoughts and words do tease my brain about a tale that I have read, wherein a Roman Emperor would seek to prove the worth of suitors through their choosing of a casket and the rightful choice must grant his daughter's hand. One such box I think shall open not upon a vessel filled with earth and worms, as the early tale does say, but on the portrait of a blinking fool, a jester's head upon a stick. For it will make my Lady clap her hands and laugh with some delight.

But now there are too many jests which make my Lady hide her face and make me sick within myself, about the Earl and getting him to bed so he may get a son, and many whisper that a man may try and do his duty and still fail at the last for the effect of too much wine. Then do they laugh and still make merry, but not in front of Oxford who seems like one in torment, and though I hate him for the harm he does us all yet I will confess there is much despair upon his face.

I have now upon me such a longing that I scarce can understand, and seeing Tannakin my heart does beat so loudly I fear the world must hear. Men jest about the way my face does colour when she touches me in passing as she has always done and I never felt this giddiness before.

DRAFT NOTES TOWARDS AN ARTICLE BY FRANCES GOODBODY

This article is intended to reflect my current researches into the family background of Edward de Vere, seventeenth Earl of Oxford 1550-1604. Although I believe that forthcoming papers by Professor R. D. Davendish will finally refute any Oxfordian claims to the authorship of Shakespeare, it is of interest to explore the spaces between historical facts.

This nobleman, tempestuous Edward of the ancient family de Vere, did not leap, fully formed in his complexities, into the spotlight of the times. A man's childhood, it is said, provides the key. So what was this man's childhood like?

His father, the sixteenth Earl, was named John. A noisy man by all accounts who relished sport and spilling blood and who entered history's Hall of Fame by cornering a wild boar in the woods of France and slaying it with a single thrust of his 'dancing rapier.' This achievement incited his companions to amazement and envy as they proclaimed the slaughterer a Hercules reborn.

His first wife was abandoned, a later mistress beaten up, a woman to whom he was engaged deserted the day before the wedding — eventually he settled down, for a dozen years or so, with Margery, the mother of Lord Edward and his sister Mary.

Margery — we know less of her but the fragments that remain are enough to chill the blood. Inspired by the teachings of sixteenth century humanists, she abided by the maxim 'cherishing marreth the sons and it utterly destroyeth the daughters.'

When Edward was twelve his father died. Margery speedily remarried and moved away, out of her son's orbit for good.

The story of another child — further on down the highway perhaps, but still on the outskirts of my explorations — Edward de Vere's daughter Elizabeth, his first child, born to his wife Anne Cecil while he was busy stamping around Europe and rejected by him as a bastard, was alienated from her father for the first five years of her life until the troubled members of the family all moved back together again.

How did she feel, this little girl, called Bess for short, growing up in her grandfather Lord Burghley's vast house? How did she cope with whispers and glances, the snide, half-heard remarks concerning bastardy, her mother Anne an unhappy shadow with her pearl of reputation smashed?

In his later years I find that Oxford took pride in his three surviving girls, Elizabeth, Bridget and Susan, and did his best to arrange good marriages for them. But Elizabeth — today we'd probably say that she 'went off the rails.' Her contemporaries described her as 'a wild girl.' Refusing to marry the Earl of Northumberland, her father's first choice of husband for her, she insisted she 'could not fancye him.' Instead, this very modern sounding girl found a man she fancied more and fell in love with William Stanley, a courtier poet, caring nothing for his lack of fortune though it must have pleased her family when he became the Earl of Derby. She married him at Greenwich with bells and songs and masques and plays.

A fairy tale come true? Definitely not. Soon the rumours started, the spies were out in force. There were tales of extravagance and wildness, an affair with the handsome Earl of Essex — the Queen's own madcap Essex — a husband jealous to the point of violence, devoted servants who pleaded her cause with their master, vowing they would leave en masse if he disowned her, (this Bess was obviously Anne Cecil's child, inspiring adoration in all who encountered her) a reconciliation, the quieter years, three children born.

AN INTERVIEW WITH T. TOWNSEND ELLIS ENTITLED 'MY HERO IN HISTORY'

INTERVIEWER: I must say at the start, Professor Ellis, that I find your choice of hero surprising. Interesting but surprising.

ELLIS: That is because you have an outmoded, romantic view of heroism. You think a hero must be a kind of demigod, a superhuman being, a doer of great deeds. That is not so. A hero is merely someone who possesses the qualities you would like to possess yourself. A role model for the individual.

INTERVIEWER: So why have you chosen William Cecil, Lord Burghley, Professor Ellis? How is he your role model?

ELLIS: I did not say he was my role model. You are putting words into my mouth.

INTERVIEWER: However there are qualities in the man that you admire …?

ELLIS: There are. He was a man of dignity, adaptable and discreet. A man to be trusted.

INTERVIEWER: A man to be trusted! Surely he was one of the most dangerous men in the kingdom. What about his spies, his network of secret agents and assassins?

ELLIS: A 'Vile Gang' as Shakespeare called them. I still say he was a man to be trusted — thriving on secret information he was as a closed book, confiding in no-one. If you tell nothing, he calculated, then there is nothing to be told. They called him The Fox since he was stealthy and lived on his wits.

INTERVIEWER: And you admire such a man? Cold and calculating …

ELLIS: I certainly do.

INTERVIEWER: Queen Elizabeth placed her trust in him. He was her good and faithful servant.

ELLIS: Exactly so. She instructed him 'Be faithful to the state without respect to my private will.' There were not many men who were allowed to overrule the great Elizabeth and ignore her tantrums!

INTERVIEWER: So he could not be corrupted?

ELLIS: I believe not. He didn't need money, being one of the richest men in the kingdom, though it must have cost him something to keep the Queen happy. He entertained her twelve times you know, on the most lavish scale.

INTERVIEWER: So what motivated him? What was the driving force behind Lord Burghley?

ELLIS: Ambition I suppose. The thirst for power. He was one of the new breed of men who would stop at nothing to achieve that.

INTERVIEWER: And you admire this quality?

ELLIS: Single mindedness is an admirable quality.

INTERVIEWER: But when it goes with total ruthlessness? However, changing the subject — he was a bit of a turncoat, wasn't he, changing allegiance many times in the early years?

ELLIS: He had no choice, if he wanted to keep his head on his shoulders. They were hazardous times, in the shadow of the block.

INTERVIEWER: So he was something of a Vicar of Bray character, a Trimmer?

ELLIS: I prefer to see him as a juggler or a card player, keeping all his options open until the last moment.

INTERVIEWER: With his eye on the main chance?

ELLIS: Certainly. Self interest was paramount. 'To thine own self be true,' that's how Shakespeare paraphrased Cecil's advice to his son.

INTERVIEWER: I always thought 'To thine own self be true,' meant something a bit more high minded, not just self interest.

ELLIS: Most people misunderstand the quotation.

INTERVIEWER: I conducted a recent interview with Professor Davendish, an expert like yourself on Shakespeare. He spoke at length about Hamlet and Polonius, saying that speech meant …

ELLIS: I am familiar with that person's theory. He is incorrect.

INTERVIEWER: I see. Now this hero of yours, Professor — he comes across a bit cold-blooded. What about the human touch? He was devoted to his family, I believe.

ELLIS: His children were of great importance to him and he had considerable respect for his wife, Mildred.

INTERVIEWER: Ah, Mildred, a most formidable lady, by all accounts.

ELLIS: Not at all. Intelligent, highly educated, efficient, single minded; an admirable woman to have as a wife.

INTERVIEWER: But there was an earlier marriage, wasn't there? A love match?

ELLIS: Cecil made a most unfortunate marriage when he was twenty-one to a girl with no dowry and a mother who kept an ale house. It was the best thing that could happen to him, her death two years later.

INTERVIEWER: Oh come, Professor! He must have been heartbroken. The girl of his dreams, married for love …

ELLIS: You talk foolishly. It would have ruined his career. Disastrous. I believe he regretted his youthful folly most bitterly and thanked God for a lucky escape.

INTERVIEWER: You are hard on your hero, Professor Ellis.

ELLIS: He was hard on himself. The only way to be. After one disastrous affair he never again let his mask slip.

INTERVIEWER: His mask … that is a good description. A man with a mask. Thank you for helping us see behind it.

ELLIS: I doubt if anyone saw behind it. He was a man who valued privacy above all else.

CORRESPONDENCE BETWEEN HENRY SHAKSPEARE AND ELLIS

Dear Professor

I am writing this in haste for my duties are pressing. I here enclose, as discussed, a copy of that section of the Earl of Oxford's letters as relates to his foreign travels 1575-1576.

I have in my possession further extracts which may be of interest to you, together with other letters which, for now, I prefer to keep to myself.

You ask whether Professor Davendish is aware of our correspondence. He is not. You may be puzzled as to my reasons for this secrecy. They are simple. These documents, the full set, are so valuable to me it is essential that only the right people see them: the people who will help me most.

I first entrusted some of these documents to Professor Davendish for I believed him our greatest living expert on the subject of Shakespearian sources. I hoped for scholarly understanding, an intellectual and systematic approach to the papers which would vindicate my claim. However, I have been disappointed. I believe there is no love lost between yourself and the Professor, so you will understand when I say he is erratic, disorganised and totally self centred. I fear he will take all credit for my story and I will be left out in the cold. As usual. His wife does her best to organise and annotate the papers but she is a most strange lady who spends a lot of time gliding round the house like a grey ghost, muttering to herself. In short, I have no faith in my employers.

However, it remains to be discussed between us how far I am willing to entrust my documents to your safe keeping. I have become mistrustful — not so much by nature as by circumstance.

Sincerely

Henry Shakspeare

Dear Mr Shakspeare

I have received the documents mentioned and noted your comments with care. My reasons for enquiring how far Professor Davendish is aware of our correspondence were simply so that I could be in full possession of the facts. If I am to be of assistance to you, I need to know such information. I trust the Professor is not aware of our negotiations. I should prefer him not to know.

Your reasons for acting as you do are your own. There is no need to reveal or explain your hostility towards your employer. I understand full well that you hold the ace in your hand and in a power game the winner must take all. There is no other way to gain control except through subterfuge.

One word of warning. Do not underrate Miss Goodbody. She may seem vague and unaware but she is of no mean ability. A lady of considerable wit — intelligence, not humour.

Please send me further documents on Oxford, particularly any that relate to his casting off of his wife. I have spent many years researching this man and though I have but little sympathy — for I find him volatile, extravagant and indiscreet — he was a complex man and I would find the key to him.

Urging upon you, once more, the need for discretion.

Ellis

Dear Professor Ellis

I enclose as requested, the documents relating to Oxford's rejection of Anne Cecil. However, I have some concerns. You admit Oxford was a complex man but show little sympathy towards him.

Of course he was volatile. Here was a passionate man full of life, an idealist, a dreamer, a man of brilliant colour trapped like a rat in a box with a tedious, old windbag of a father-in-law on one side and a weeping, timid, pale faced wife on the other. No wonder he broke out. He was a chameleon playing change and change about to suit the game, but when he travelled, when he escaped, he found what he was missing. There is no way he can be excused for his shocking treatment of Anne Cecil, but he was desperate.

You may wonder why I should defend Oxford's personality and actions when my purpose is the vindication of Gilbert Shakespeare as author. These people may be dead but they are all real to me. Every last one. They are my heritage.

Henry Shakspeare.

Dear Mr Shakspeare

I received your letter and the documents referred to. My thanks.

I am many years your senior and highly regarded in my field. I do not expect a young man to tell me what to think.

I fear Mr Shakspeare, that you are projecting. Could it be that it is not Oxford's feelings you are describing but your own?

I must urge you to beware of this temptation. Let the facts speak for themselves. Trust in research; that at least will not betray you. Curb your passion. A cool head may succeed but an emotional heart never will.

Send me the letters. I do not need your comments. Be discreet, confide in no-one. Keep your secrets if you wish; I know that you will come to me in the end. Keep a close check on all your feelings else you will never be anything but a little man ranting and raving while the great ones laugh.

Ellis

'HOURS AND LONG HOURS'

"What does he mean?" muttered Henry to himself, re-reading Ellis's last, curt letter. "Projecting my own emotions on to Oxford? The man's mad."

He tossed the letter to one side and sat down at his desk. At least he could follow one part of Ellis's advice and trust in research.

The windows in Henry's bedroom, where he liked to work, overlooked the back garden. There had been an unexpected September frost in the night and the grass was stiff, glittery and white. It reminded him of many mornings during his childhood in the Fens when he would drag back the curtains and there would be a whole white world. He wished he was there now, by those sodden fields and rivers, with the smell of fish in the air and the cries of wild geese. He would have been a Fen Tiger, he thought, in those long ago days, a half-savage outlaw wading through swamps or manoeuvering a small boat from island to island, ready to defend his wild and flooded land from those who would consume it.

He pulled his books and notepad towards him then paused, his attention caught by a ginger cat in the garden creeping over the frosty lawn.

No good reminiscing. He was far away from his beloved Fenland now and there was work to be done.

He read through the notes he had already made on Oxford. After his tour of the Strand and Covent Garden he had managed to describe his impressions of imagined life in Cecil House and had written, somewhat lyrically for him, about the silvery Thames with its echoes of music and church bells in the air. A world of gold plate and fine clothes: that was what Oxford and his entourage would have known. The other world, the one from which Gilbert Shakespeare had been rescued, was a terrifying place of dirt and disease, with household rubbish, dead dogs and human excrement dumped along the city walls in ditches and the lower reaches of the Thames itself. All this filth would have been scraped up at night by gong farmers and rakers, loaded on to barges and disposed of somewhere outside the city.

'However,' he wrote, 'Oxford and the rest of his family cannot have been unaware of this world of sewage and smell, especially if they had sensitive noses like their Queen. After all, this was why the occupants of great houses moved out every few months, so that 'the sweetening' could take place: fresh rushes, fragrant with rosemary and herbs, would be scattered on the floors and the old grasses, thick with mud, scraps of food and droppings, be cleared away as compost. Cardinal Wolsey certainly knew what he was about at Hampton Court when he ordered his palace to be fitted with expensive, new-fangled carpeting.'

Henry stopped writing and listened. The house was unusually quiet: no music from the kitchen radio, no telephone ringing in the hall. Frances was away in Brighton, giving a talk on John Keats as part of her Victorian Poets series. He considered going downstairs to make some tea and toast to warm himself up but was anxious not to bump into Ardie. It was becoming more and more impossible to be under the same roof as the man. A clash of personalities, he supposed, but his employer made him feel swamped, drained of energy and sucked dry as if by a vampire. Henry smiled. Ardie was not Dracula. He didn't mean that. He was just overwhelming. Charismatic and charming as the Professor might be, with a razor sharp intellect and a brilliance with words, Henry thought him a dominating man and totally self-absorbed.

The ginger cat was hiding behind a shrub, watching a blackbird pecking for worms in the hard soil. Henry tapped on the glass to alert it to danger and the cat fled with its fur bushed up.

"Not long," he said to himself, staring at the calendar on his desk and trying to calculate days. Many times he found himself dreaming about Christmas — not the ghosts of Christmas Past, those were best forgotten, but about the Christmas soon to come, by which time the important presentation in Cambridge would have taken place and he himself would be far away from Midhurst and the Davendish household — miles away if he could fix it, making sure that Felix, the most important person in his life, his main responsibility, was taken care of. By then, with luck, all his claims would at last be believed, Gilbert Shakespeare recognised as the true author and he — Henry hardly dared imagine what the future might hold for him next.

He glanced at Ellis' letter again, frowning at its abrupt tone. How could anyone think he had much in common with Oxford — a handsome, extrovert adventurer who rejoiced in defying both man and God and mocked his enemies even as they hurled accusation after accusation against him. Henry had read some of these denouncements: Oxford, they said, had called the Virgin Mary a whore and Joseph a cuckold. Even more damaging, the Earl had been overheard making insulting comments about the Queen's singing voice and passing on snide remarks about her clothes. Dangerous talk. All this in addition to accusations of promiscuity, sodomy, drunkenness and theft.

Henry took a deep breath. There was no way he had ever skated on such thin ice, even in his most defiant, rebellious years.

He picked up his pen again and started writing rapidly, anxious to be done. 'The Earl of Oxford was noted for his prodigious extravagance, much of it spent on rich apparel, the rest on foreign travel. He was an extravagant man in every sense — 'a lusty gentleman' in the words of one chronicler of the time.'

Oxford's appearance mattered so much to him, thought Henry as he got up to add another jumper to the layers he was already wearing. His room was getting chillier by the minute. He considered his own bleak wardrobe: his clothes would fit, with room to spare, into a small holdall — years of living in the damp Fens had made him impervious to anything but the need for warmth and waterproofing. But Oxford — he thought nothing of tossing away a small fortune on velvet and satin. Even when he was sick and feverish one year and sent by Burghley to a sweat house in Windsor to recover or die, he was still sending his servant out for a new doublet and fine hose, as well as for cakes and ale and books. Henry sympathised with the need for books: they could be the best of companions in the lonely hours, but as for the rest, it meant nothing to him.

'Whatever the treatment in this hothouse, the young man was soon back on form,' wrote Henry returning to his desk.

'We hear about him not long afterwards, orchestrating a mock combat at Warwick Castle for the delight of his Queen — a combat that involved two armies of courtiers dressed as soldiers, battering rams and gigantic fireballs, some of which rolled down the castle hill into the Avon, setting light to floating rafts of wood and tar and lighting up the whole night sky. The finale of this spectacle was a monstrous man-made dragon shooting out flames and turning several nearby houses into an inferno — at which point Edward de Vere and his brave soldiers rushed to the rescue, dousing the flames. Whether the compensation paid from the Queen's coffers was enough to recompense one man for the hole in his roof 'as big as a man's head' we do not know. It is unlikely to have comforted the family who saw two of its members die in the blaze.'

Henry pushed back his chair abruptly and stood up. Enough was enough of this Elizabethan land of sewage and perfume. The whole of that year, 1572, while Oxford was playing the pyromaniac, had been one of flames in the sky and sudden death, with thousands of Huguenots slaughtered in the tinderbox of Paris — news which the King of Spain had greeted with pleasure, calling it one of the greatest joys of his life.

Downstairs, Ardie was moving about in the kitchen, opening the back door, tapping a plate loudly and calling the cat in for its breakfast.

'I've finished with Oxford,' thought Henry, shuffling his papers together. 'Someone else can do the research if they want. Gilbert Shakespeare's the only one I care about, proving his claim and mine.'

He tugged on his jacket and picked up his keys quietly. Pepys, he recalled, had visited the Fens and written about it in his diary. He had found it damp, misty and miserable but made himself snug by a friend's fire that evening, both of them telling each other three good ghost stories before bed. Henry smiled as he crept downstairs. He had a story to tell, much better than any of Samuel Pepys.

'THAT I MAY WATCH'

"Thank you very much, Professor Ellis," said the presenter. "I am sure your comments on the relevance of Shakespeare to the youth of today give us all plenty to think about."

Ellis stared firmly into the camera and nodded slightly.

"Thank you." He smiled modestly. "It is important for those of us who consider ourselves authorities on the subject of Shakespeare to keep on the same wavelength as our young people. They, after all, are the ones who will carry on the traditions, bringing fresh and modern insights to the subject."

"Silly old fool," muttered Ardie, glaring at the TV screen. "Trying to act all modern. He wouldn't know a wavelength if it tripped him up!"

Frances glanced anxiously at her husband. His face was red and there were beads of sweat. He had been very good so far, muttering quietly to himself and snorting with contempt as Ellis spoke, but it was beginning to get out of control. It rankled, far more than he would admit, that he had not been included in the Forum. This, in spite of the producer's abject apologies when Ardie had phoned him up two days previously.

"I have to hear about it from some young whipper-snapper of a reporter," he yelled down the telephone, "asking me if it is true I am making no more public appearances. Me! I'll have you know that I am considered by those who understand these things to be the greatest living authority on Shakespeare in the world! Professor Ellis knows nothing compared to me. Nothing!"

The producer of the programme had stemmed this tide of fury eventually, promising a special debate after Christmas with Ardie as guest speaker.

"I do assure you, Professor Davendish," he continued smoothly, "that had it not been for reliable information that you were out of the country, you would naturally have been our first choice on this occasion."

"I don't know where you got that so called reliable information from," said Ardie, slightly mollified. "I certainly haven't got time to go abroad at the moment. I am working on some very important research you know. It is all highly confidential, but I'll tell you this much …" his voice dropped to a whisper, "when my findings are published, they will stun the world. I tell you straight, you and your ilk will come crawling to me then, begging me to fill your silly little air spaces. You wait." His voice rose in triumph and he beamed at his reflection in a mirror, oblivious to Henry who was coming down the stairs muttering 'Me! Me! Me!'

Frances felt a guilty sense of relief that Ardie wasn't going to be on television. The torment of watching her husband reveal himself in temper, folly and pride was too awful to bear. She watched Ellis on the screen. He was calm, dignified, unruffled, exuding intelligence and charm. He was as arrogant as Ardie, as calculating and unscrupulous, but he never let it show in public. His mask was always firmly in place. Ardie, on the other hand, had only to open his mouth to become a caricature of himself.

"Professor Ellis," said the Forum presenter, "I wonder if, before we finish, you would be kind enough to give us an update on the controversy surrounding the authorship of Shakespeare. Where do you stand in this debate? For instance, do you go along with theories about Bacon or Marlowe, is it still the conventionally accepted Man of Stratford or do you uphold the currently fashionable view that the real playwright was Edward de Vere, the Earl of Oxford?"

Ellis leaned forward, gazing intensely into the camera. His pale blue eyes were clear.

"This is a mystery," he said softly, "that has fascinated people for centuries, virtually since the plays were first written. It is the greatest puzzle of all time, a far greater mystery than who murdered the Princes in the Tower or who was Jack the Ripper. Trying to discover the identity of Shakespeare is like going through a maze with a blindfold on, like reading a whodunit with the last chapter missing." Ellis shook his head as if to clear his thoughts. "There can be no doubt that the name of the real author was deliberately shrouded in secrecy. A political cover up. A cruel plot to obliterate the identity of the greatest genius the world has ever known. There can be no doubt that the real author of the plays and sonnets was the Earl of Oxford."

"Rubbish!" shouted Ardie at the screen.

"Professor Ellis," said the presenter, "I know I am about to ask the impossible, but can you briefly, in a few sentences, tell us why you are so convinced that William Shakespeare of Stratford was not the real author, in spite of generations of people believing that he was?"

Ellis closed his eyes for a second. "Briefly, William of Stratford was unimportant. There is no hard proof to link his identity with that of the author. All claims to the contrary are based on unverified hearsay, false assumptions and inconsistent evidence."

"Gently, my dear," said Frances to her husband who was groaning loudly and tugging at his hair. "He's nearly finished. We've always known that Ellis is an Oxfordian. He's not saying anything new."

"Finally," said the presenter, "I wonder if you could, with the same admirable brevity, sum up for us your conviction that the Earl of Oxford wrote the plays."

Ellis smiled charmingly. "The man who wrote Shakespeare was a man with a brilliant mind. Highly literate and educated, a man with an intimate knowledge of the Elizabethan court, of politics, of foreign travel, of the law courts, of archery, falconry, warfare ..." He paused. "Need I go on? I could for hours. There is no way the Man of Stratford could have possessed the tiniest portion of these skills. As his will shows, he didn't appear to have any books to leave to his family. Evidence seems to suggest his daughter was illiterate. On the other hand, a person like Oxford — educated in Burghley's household from the age of twelve, married to his daughter — was uniquely placed to be such a man."

"Then who distorted the evidence?" said the presenter, looking dazed. "Who was responsible for this cover up you talk about?"

"Lord Burghley himself. The whole Cecil family. Possibly the Queen herself. You mustn't forget," said Ellis gently to the presenter who was staring open mouthed, "that it was not a common or a reputable thing in those days for a nobleman to write plays. Besides, Cecil hated his son-in-law and Oxford hated him. The plays are full of jokes and skits against the Cecil family. The Elizabethans would have spotted them instantly and had a good laugh. It really is no wonder the Cecils wanted the man's identity kept secret. The extraordinary thing is that they succeeded. Until now, that is."

"Until now," echoed the presenter.

Ellis stared into the camera as if looking for someone. He smiled triumphantly.

"Ardie," said Frances anxiously, as her husband buried his face in his hands, "please …"

He stood up. His hair was wet and his face shining with perspiration but his eyes were bright with joy.

"Got him!" he shouted. "We've got him! By his own words he's trapped himself. He's dug himself a pit and fallen into it."

"What do you mean?" cried Frances. "I didn't hear Ellis say anything foolish."

"No," shouted Ardie, pacing up and down the room with excitement, "he didn't say anything foolish. He spoke the truth, as much of it as he knows. But he admitted … admitted …" Ardie paused, gasping for breath.

"Slowly, my dear," whispered Frances. "Tell me quietly what Ellis admitted."

Ardie mopped his brow. "He admitted that someone brought up in the household of William Cecil, Lord Burghley, was uniquely placed to be the real author."

"Yes, I heard him say that. You mean …?"

"I mean that for once Ellis was right. The real author was brought up in the Cecil household. Only it wasn't Oxford as

that fool Ellis thinks. We know it was Gilbert Shakespeare."
Ardie smiled triumphantly. "Wait till he finds out how near the
truth he was. And on television too. The greatest mystery the
world has ever known he said. When he learns that I've done
it, that I'm the one to find the missing bit of the jigsaw, it will
kill him."

Henry, who had been sitting at the back of the room all
during the television programme, slipped out quietly and went
up to his room. There he pulled an old tin chest out from
under his bed, unlocked it with the key which he wore, night
and day around his neck, and gently lifted out a very faded
letter. Slowly he walked over to the window, reading again in
the half-light the words he knew by heart.

"You've got the missing bit of the jigsaw, have you?" he
whispered. "That's what you think." He gave a short laugh.
"There's something about Gilbert Shakespeare that even you
don't know."

He put the letter away carefully then, pulling on his coat,
went out into the town. The curfew bell in the church tower
was striking eight o'clock as if calling all lost travellers home.
Henry made his way purposefully towards the telephone
kiosk.

JOURNAL OF GILBERT SHAKESPEARE

OCTOBER 1582

This night am I damned to hell for all eternity and my limbs so shake with fear and guilt that I can scarcely write. Though I burn in fire and torment ever after, yet tonight I am consumed with joy and cannot think it such a terrible thing to lose my soul for this.

For fear of discovery I dare not write overmuch though I long to tell the world that she, who I love more than life itself, loves me also, and clinging to me in despair and loneliness and pain, did lay with me this night in such warmth and sweet longing that, though I did protest for her reputation's sake, I was as one entranced and could not prevent myself. And though I did cry out in agony that surely she was blind, that surely she must find me a repulsive and loathsome thing for my deformity, yet did she stop my mouth with kisses and swear she loved me for my true heart.

Now God knows what pain for us lies ahead, and though I care not for myself yet will I protect her until my dying hour for the honour she has done me. I count myself the richest man on earth and the proudest and whatever comes there is nothing can spoil the joy of this most joyous night.

NOTES BY FRANCES ON THE BOYHOOD OF GILBERT SHAKESPEARE

There are problems here if we intend pushing the claim of Gilbert Shakespeare to be the sole author of the collected works. Hopefully some of these points may be clarified.

The main argument against William of Stratford is that he was uneducated and had no way of acquiring the skills necessary for the authorship. Without going into these issues, for there is considerable disagreement, we need to see how far Gilbert fits into the pattern.

We are so limited in our evidence. All we have is a handful of letters from various people and some extracts from a journal. Much of our proof must be based on surmise. However, I feel no compunction in doing this; whole volumes, learned volumes, have been written about William Shakespeare and we know even less about him. Likewise, many experts have written treatises proving Oxford to have been the man. We know more about his life, but there is no hard evidence that he was the author.

What would Gilbert have needed if he was to write these plays and sonnets? A good education, an exceptional education. You may be born a genius but you are not born speaking Latin. So where did our little tumbling boy acquire such knowledge? Lord Burghley owned several magnificent houses, each one stacked with libraries ceiling-high with erudite books — Ovid, Plutarch, Boccaccio, Chaucer, Holinshed, Geoffrey of Monmouth — tome after weighty tome of famous names. Anne Cecil may have taught the boy a lot herself, as children down the ages have loved playing schools, but would that have been enough? Anne's mother, Mildred, was one of the most learned ladies in the land and would have been bound to insist on an excellent education for her only daughter, but Anne's education, though good, would still have been incomplete, curtailed by an early marriage — and passed on to a little boy? — it doesn't seem enough. The author was brilliantly educated; computer programmes have been devised that show the extent of his knowledge and the immensity of his vocabulary.

Our theory is that Gilbert acquired all this knowledge during the 'missing' years from 1576 to 1581. During these years Anne was living apart from her husband. But she didn't live alone. She lived with her parents and it is likely that Gilbert was with her. Her devotion to him shines out of every word she wrote and I believe that during these years she persuaded her father to have her favourite educated along with his Wards. He had done the same for Oxford and there was no way William Cecil could have resisted the least wish of his daughter.

So I believe that Gilbert Shakespeare received a first class education in those years. We know the curriculum laid down for Burghley's Wards:

7.00-7.30	Dancing
7.30-8.00	Breakfast
8.00-9.00	French
9.00-10.00	Latin
10.00-10.30	Writing and Drawing
1.00-2.00	Cosmography
2.00-3.00	Latin
3.00-4.00	French
4.00-4.30	Exercises with the pen.
Evening	Prayers and Dinner

Some days off for riding, shooting, walking etc.

Add to this the knowledge of botanical terms that Shakespeare shows — his plays and sonnets are full of floral imagery — these he could have gained from many hours spent in Cecil's superb gardens.

What else did Shakespeare need to know? The language of politics, an inside knowledge of the power game, the language and emotion of ambition, intrigue and policy. Gilbert had plenty of opportunity to observe and learn from living with the Cecils; a little boy slowly growing up to be a man and all the while watching, overhearing every whisper, living on his wits for his self-appointed task — the protection of the Lady Anne.

What about the knowledge of law? Oxford studied at the Inns of Court and often brought companions home, drunken probably, loquacious in their cups, enough to give a little boy a wealth of information to be stored away for later use.

What about the lovers, the hints of kinky sex, the Dark Lady. Is that Anne? There is no tangible evidence of Anne in the well-known plays, all of which seem to have been written in the years after her death in 1588. She may, of course, have been the model for Ophelia as many people believe and there are the famous love sonnets. Other sonnets, however, reveal only bitterness, disgust, contempt for women and the sexual act. I will concede I have no neat answer for this — let other theorists try and discover more and show us Gilbert's later life; there was no way he would allow any hint of Tannakin to creep into his verse. In death, as in life, he would protect her name — and passion, real passion, died with her.

'TO DELIGHT THE WORLD'

In Parham House, an Elizabethan mansion in West Sussex, there is a seventeenth century portrait by Sir Peter Lely of a young woman with her husband. There the latter stands, like a study in arrogance, with one boot on the hem of his wife's gown, holding her long hair firmly between finger and thumb.

Frances, feeling herself haunted by the portrait, studied the girl's face. Lely had painted the girl's soul in her very eyes. Was this how Anne looked, she wondered, haunted and lost, with all her love twisted and turned back on her like a slap in the face from a cold cod?

The guide came into the room.

"Can you tell me," said Frances, smiling at the woman, "about one of the paintings over there? That one ..."

"Elizabeth Harrington," said the guide without even looking. "It always is."

Frances stared in amazement. "I mean the one of the girl with the man holding her hair and standing on ..."

"Elizabeth Harrington," said the guide again. "You don't need to describe it to me. It's the only picture they always ask about. Especially the women visitors. Some of them get really angry and upset about it. You can buy a postcard downstairs," she added helpfully.

Frances nodded. "I can see why it makes women angry. Do you know the background to it?"

"Elizabeth ran away from her husband but was brought back. He had the portrait of the two of them painted, as a reminder I suppose, or a warning."

"Did she ever try and run away again?"

The guide shook her head. "By all accounts they lived happily ever after."

Frances stared at her in horror. "What, after the way he humiliated her? Had her painted like that for all to see? I don't believe they can have been happy!"

The woman nodded. "That's what the books in the library here say. They certainly had lots of children."

"That proves nothing," muttered Frances.

She wandered round the formally laid out gardens of the house, bright in the colours that only late September could bring, thinking of the women who had lived in those days. Women of wealth with titles and lands and hunting dogs. Beneath their elaborate gowns of satin and silk and corsets that dug the very breath out of them, they were frequently pregnant. The years of fertility were many and long.

'The deaths were worse,' thought Frances, gazing unseeingly at the herb garden. 'So many babies and so many died.'

She had once mentioned the subject of Elizabethan infant mortality to Ardie.

"Oh I expect they got used to it," he said, casually.

'Never,' thought Frances, wandering across the lawns to the lake and leaning on the bridge, 'you'd never get used to your babies dying.'

Underneath the bridge little clouds of smoke came puffing out at intervals and there was a soft hissing noise. Frances peered down but couldn't find the cause. 'Probably a dragon,' she thought. She wandered on past the tiny church in the grounds where for centuries the owners of Parham had worshipped in their own pew with a fireplace to keep the family warm. As she gazed across the park a group of stags on the skyline of the hill looked distantly back at her and she could hear the ducks quacking loudly on the lake. When the season started, thought Frances, the grounds would be thrown open for a privileged few and the ducks shot for sport.

"Ardie," said Frances, walking into her husband's study, fed up with knocking at an unanswered door. "I want to ask you about Gilbert Shakespeare."

Ardie, nodding off in his armchair, jerked awake and glared at his wife. "What do you mean by barging in here? I don't want anything!"

"No," said Frances, "but I do. Besides which I am your wife and I live here and if I wish to walk into one of my own rooms to talk to my own husband, then I think I am entitled. Elizabeth Harrington ran away for less," she added, as Ardie stared, open mouthed.

"Well, what do you want then?" he said. "I've got a lot of work to do you know."

"Quite so," said Frances. "I have too. I've been typing up some of the letters and journals and I keep coming across references to Gilbert Shakespeare and some disability he had. He goes on about it all the time, right from the start when he was a child and his family threw him out because of it, up to the very moment when he goes to bed with Anne and he's frantic in case this mysterious handicap turns her off."

She paused and studied her husband who was looking very smug. "I wondered if you wanted me to write up some notes on Elizabethan ailments and possible handicaps, in case you get questioned at Cambridge about it all. However, since you're looking like the cat that got the cream I suppose you know the answer already."

Her husband smiled. "Well" he said, "I do have a theory. You really needn't worry yourself. You might know that I would come up with the answer."

"I should have guessed you would," said Frances, sinking down into a chair and preparing herself to be lectured at. Once Ardie was in full swing there was no stopping him.

"What do you think was the nature of poor Gilbert's disability then?"

Ardie rose to his feet. He strode up and down the room three times, hands behind his back, stopped in front of one of his tall bookshelves, ran his fingers across the spines of the covers until he found the book he wanted, opened it, rustled through the pages with a frown, read something softly to himself, tossed the book on the armchair, cleared his throat and turned in the direction of his wife, gazing over the top of her head at something in a distant space only he could see. Frances waited patiently for the performance to begin. She had been a spectator many times before.

"In my opinion," began Ardie, "the existence of his handicap grieved Gilbert Shakespeare deeply. It affected his outlook, his attitudes, his relationships, his view of himself. It was the dark side of his life. He saw himself as twisted, as warped, different to other men. This man, who we now know was the real author of the Shakespeare works, drew deeply on his experiences as source material for his plays. It is my belief," cried Ardie in a loud voice, "that in the persona of Richard III, Gilbert Shakespeare depicted himself."

Frances resisted the temptation to put her hand up like a little girl.

"He was a hunchback then?" she asked softly.

Ardie glanced at her impatiently. "No, I don't suppose for a moment that Gilbert was a hunchback. It's only hammy actors that have given the public this idea that Richard III was a hunchback. Modern research inclines more to the view that it was polio or some other ailment in childhood that gave the man a minor deformity, one shoulder slightly higher than the other, wasted muscles, something like that. That is my theory."

Frances nodded slowly, thinking hard. "So you think it was something like polio with Gilbert? I get the impression it was more than that. He was so wretched about it all his life and his own parents threw him out into the streets because of it …"

"They would do," said Ardie, walking over to the door. "They couldn't afford to keep a sick child, could they? Anyone who didn't fit in or had something wrong with them was out. They were cruel times, you know they were. You'll have to excuse me Frances, I need to make a phone call."

He disappeared into the hallway and a few minutes later Frances heard him talking on the telephone. She sighed heavily. Cruel times they certainly were, but had anything much changed? Television had brought all the horrors of the world into her own home. There was no escaping it any longer. Compared with some of the atrocities she saw daily, the plight of a little boy turned out into the streets because he was ill and ugly, the agony of women of child-bearing years burying baby after baby, didn't seem so important. Frances stood up briskly. Of course it was important. It was all relative. Pain hurt whatever the time or place. The only way to survive was not to think too much. No wonder Shakespeare's Lear had gone mad, baring his head to the elements and his soul to reality.

As she turned to go out of the room she paused for a moment studying the books on Ardie's 'special' shelf. His publications. The written proof that R. D. Davendish was a famous man. Someone who had made it. A man to be envied. Theory after theory, there they all were, lined up along the shelf like children in a Victorian household brought down at the end of the day for inspection by their papa. So many books and articles. Frances peered short-sightedly at the titles: The Identity of the Dark Lady in the Shakespearian Sonnet, Images of Falconry in the Shakespearian Play, The Symbolism of Angling: an examination of three Shakespearian plays, Cyphers and Codes in Shakespeare's Last Sonnets. Frances paused at the last one: that had almost been Ardie's undoing. He had attempted to decipher a code in the sonnets that would have proved the Bard to have been a secret agent along with Kit Marlowe. Ardie claimed with a shout that both men had been murdered.

"Crank," yelled back Ellis in every literary journal and media programme. "Ravings of a lunatic." Ellis was so happy that year, remembered Frances, scoring one over Ardie.

She made her way slowly up the stairs to her bedroom, feeling very old and tired. That was what had done it she thought, smashed the one time friendship of her two dearest friends. Not the rivalry over her, bitter though it had been; neither Ardie nor Ellis were the sort to be scarred for life for love of a woman. No, it was the backbiting, the years of erosion.

Frances sank down on her bed. Ardie would be waiting for his dinner, Henry would be expecting the promised typing to be finished. But she couldn't be bothered to do anything.

"Damn Gilbert Shakespeare and all his crew," she exclaimed. "It's the missing letters we really need."

She got to her feet and pulled down a big cardboard box off the top of her wardrobe.

"What if someone was writing about us? Me and Ardie and Ellis. I bet there won't be more than half a dozen letters from all those years."

The box was covered in dust. She opened it carefully. Inside there were photographs in plenty, sepia coloured for the best part — Ardie and Ellis as children in Ipswich growing up together, Ardie and Ellis at Eton, handsome and arrogant, dozens of pictures of Ardie and Ellis at Cambridge, Ardie in his car, herself and Ardie leaning out of the car waving, a political rally with Ardie thumping the platform against Fascism, a political meeting with Ellis standing, dignified as ever, preaching pacifism, herself and Ellis by the river, herself standing outside Ellis's flat gazing upwards dreamily, herself and Ardie holding hands, the three of them together, linked and laughing, their wedding with herself looking scared and Ellis a grim best man.

After the wedding there didn't seem to be any more photographs in the box. Frances, rifling through it, found only a few letters. None were from Ellis. Hadn't he written any letters in those years? Did he, like Lord Burghley, believe that if you told nothing there was nothing to tell? Had she imagined the love then? Certainly there was no evidence. Even Ardie, a most passionate man in the early years, seemed not to have committed any of it to paper.

'Well then,' thought Frances, 'perhaps it was all a dream. It was so long ago and we are all old.'

She unfolded a final scrap of paper and smiled to herself as she read the short note. No love letter really, but something scribbled by Ardie. They had been married a couple of months, to judge by the date on the letter and she, feeling queasy from pregnancy, had gone up to Wales to stay with her mother. Ardie, still in Cambridge, had written from there:

My dearest Frances,

Hope you are feeling a bit better and the journey didn't make you sick. Frantically busy so can't write much. Cambridge pretty gloomy at the moment with this wretched war. Still feel torn, what with being needed here and wanting to go and fight Jerry. Lots of memorial services in the chapels, very grim and all lights out in the streets at night. King's Chapel would be a sitting duck. Cambridge looks quite medieval in the gloom.

More cheerful things. I'm doing the flat up so you'll have a great surprise and when the baby's born you won't have to worry about doing anything to the place. Tried to get Ellis to help but he's not talking to me at the moment. Sick with envy I suppose because I won you. Teach him to be quicker off the mark.

Knowing you like green stuff, I happened to go into the Co-op and there they had rolls and rolls of lino, a bargain, so I said I'd have the lot and they're going to lay it tomorrow. So hurry up and come home and you'll see how nice the whole place looks in dark green.

Got to go now. In the middle of an article about herbal medicines in Shakespeare. Got this amazing idea about it all. Think Ellis has got wind of it so won't say too much at present.

Come back soon. Need you here. Know you're safe in Wales but can't wait for you to see the lino.

R x

Frances folded the faded letter slowly and put it back in the box. She smiled as she walked back downstairs to start the dinner. She remembered the day she saw that green lino. As she walked into the flat she had been greeted by the sight of brown. Everywhere. The whole house, every patch of floor. The colour matched the existing brown paintwork.

"I thought you said the lino was green!" she said in horror.

"It is," said Ardie, surprised. "Don't you like it then?"

That was the first time Frances realised that Ardie was colour blind. As the years passed, she found there were other kinds of blindness.

'NO MORE LAPIS'

One Saturday, as a late October evening grew dark and chilly and hints of Hallowe'en were in the air, Frances parked her car in the grounds of the school — not the old Grammar at the gateway of the town overlooking the proud Horse Chestnut and the ancient Copper Beech, but a residential establishment a few miles further out: a school for children with educational problems. This building, converted from an old manor house, set amidst green hills, vast lawns and bushes of azaleas and rhododendrons, housed many of the County's troubled children.

Henry, having watched some of the children making a camp in the undergrowth, began to walk down the drive in the direction of the car park and so had the advantage of glimpsing Frances before she saw him. This way he had ten seconds to decide whether to stay or retreat into the woods. He stayed where he was.

"Why Henry," said Frances, as she saw the silent figure watching her, "fancy seeing you!" She walked slowly towards him. "What brings you here?"

"I am visiting my son," said Henry.

Frances nodded. It was all in keeping, she thought, with the events of the last crazy months. This latest bit of information seemed almost logical. Yes, Henry would have a son. Yes, he would be here in a school for the disturbed and the handicapped. It was another piece in the jigsaw, another thread in the story that was weaving its way tighter and tighter round their lives.

"I am a governor here," she said. "I like to visit regularly but I've been busy. I thought I knew all the children though, at least by name, but I don't remember coming across one called Shakspeare ... I'm sure I'd have noticed ..."

"He hasn't been here long," said Henry curtly. "Only since I had the dubious pleasure of working for your husband. In any case my son hasn't got the same name as me. He bears his mother's name, Pettifer. I see no reason to change it. Yet."

A car coming down the long drive made them move out of the way. With one accord they walked back through the trees towards the sounds of the children playing in the undergrowth.

"There he is," said Henry, stopping by a fallen tree trunk.

Frances saw a boy with dark hair standing slightly apart from the rest. The last rays of sunlight flickering through the trees dappled the shadows in the clearing and fell across the boy's face. He was smiling.

"He looks happy," she said.

"Oh he's happy enough," said Henry. He turned and stared at Frances. "You might be happier than you are Miss Goodbody, if your brain had been damaged at birth."

Frances tried not to flinch. "I'm sure I would."

Henry glared at her. "Is that all you can say?"

Frances sat down wearily on the tree trunk. "If I told you I was sorry or showed any kind of sympathy, you'd curse me as a hypocrite or a middle-class phoney or something of the kind. I'm sorry that your child is brain damaged, that you are so unhappy, that you and my husband seem to have become enemies and you've moved out of my house, that you are determined to damage him somehow."

She paused and stared back at Henry. "I am very sorry not to have known you properly. You lived with us for three months and I didn't even know you had a child. That is very sad."

From the main building someone was calling. The children left their half-made camp and began wandering back in twos and threes. As Henry's son walked dreamily past them, Frances reached out and touched his hand. The boy turned his head slowly and stared at her. His eyes were a deep brown and empty.

"Introduce me to your son, Henry," said Frances.

He gave an impatient sigh. "This is my son, Felix Pettifer, aged thirteen. Felix, this is Miss Goodbody, a very important lady."

"I'm not important," said Frances, "but I am very pleased to meet you."

He stared at her then walked off towards the house.

"He is beautiful, Henry," said Frances. "Why did you call him Felix?"

"His mother's name was Felicity. He's named after her. Felicity means joy." He laughed grimly.

"Was?" said Frances. "Is she dead then?"

"As good as," he said, watching a small frog hopping across the leaves.

"You don't have to tell me," said Frances.

"Not a lot to tell. I met her when I was eighteen and fell for her in a big way. She thought it was a good laugh going around with me — she always did like shocking people and it gave her a thrill to see their expressions when they met me for the first time and pretended not to notice my face." He rubbed his hand across the livid birthmark. "She said it turned her on, kissing a man with a twisted mouth. She was more than a bit twisted herself I think. She got pregnant, but exhibitionist that she was she made a great thing of dragging me out in public, hanging round my neck and kissing me wildly whenever anyone was looking, and all the time wearing skin-tight dresses and flaunting her great big belly." He sighed deeply. "It was all for show. When we were alone she kicked and spat, and swore she had always loathed the sight of me and, in spite of her condition, she started sleeping with every Tom, Dick and Harry."

He clenched his fists. Frances sat still, not daring to move.

"She started going to this Catholic priest, begging for help and doing the Mary Magdalene bit — but it was another one of her tricks. She was going around openly boasting how she was determined to get him, and she did — the poor fool was quite besotted with her and she was in her element, shocking everyone. She persuaded him to go off with her for a couple of nights, and her all of eight months pregnant with my kid, and there was a car smash and the bloody priest was killed instantly and she was rushed into hospital with a shattered spine. Felix was delivered a few hours later. The result you've seen." He paused and took a deep breath. "She's been paralysed from the neck down ever since. That's my story, Miss Goodbody, for what it's worth."

The frog crept under the leaves. Frances rubbed her eyes.

156

"Somewhere there's a pattern, Henry. There must be a pattern, a meaning to all these stories."

They were both silent. The moon had crept over the trees and the clearing was full of a white light.

"Henry," said Frances, "if you succeed in what you're doing, in getting Gilbert Shakespeare recognised, will you change his name to yours? Felix, I mean. Will it make it all worthwhile?"

Henry shook his head. "Nothing will make it worthwhile. I thought it would when I started all this. I was full of hope in the summer. But what good will it do Felix to know he is the last living descendant of Shakespeare? He's never heard of the man, will never be able to read any of his works, will never in all his lifetime share the faintest flicker of the man's visions. It's all wasted, Miss Goodbody. All wasted."

They walked slowly back to the cars.

"I'm sure Felix has his own dreams," said Frances. "They may not have the power of Shakespeare's visions but they are still real."

He shook his head. "He doesn't."

They paused and looked back at the old building that was the boys' dormitory.

"He'll be asleep up there soon," said Henry, "cuddling his teddy bear and sucking his thumb. I know. I've seen him."

"There's worse things," said Frances. "He's only thirteen."

"He'll be the same when he's thirty. Or sixty. Or ninety. He'll always need looking after. If nothing else I've got to get enough money from this Shakespeare business to see him taken care of for the rest of his life."

"Don't worry about the money," said Frances. "I've got a book coming out soon; it should be a bestseller. He can have some of the money from that — lots of it — all of it if you like! I was only going to buy a car ... this is more important."

"I wouldn't consider it!" said Henry. "He's my son and it's my job to take care of him. It's my fault that all this happened."

"Is that true? You arranged for the car smash did you? You arranged for his mother to be crippled and your child damaged, did you? You are cleverer than I thought."

"No! I never wanted any of those things to happen. Felicity didn't get herself pregnant on her own, whatever her games. Some of the responsibility is mine."

"It's called the life force, Henry," said Frances, unlocking her car. "The urge to re-create oneself. The desire to see offspring of our line. It's very common. In your case, with your famous name, I would have said it was inevitable."

She started the motor. The engine came to life with a loud roar that shook the silent grounds.

"I meant what I said, Henry," said Frances, leaning out of the window. "You must let me help. Please. I shall arrange it with my solicitors. Felix shall be taken care of, I promise you."

He came and stood close to the car so she couldn't reverse, bending down so that their faces were almost touching.

"Are you interfering, Miss Goodbody? Are you being a do-gooder, Miss Goodbody?" He smiled bitterly and the mark on his face twisted. "But what if I am not worth it? What then, Miss Goodbody?"

"I know what you are, Henry. I know that my husband's arrogance has driven you wild and that you and Ellis between you are planning to destroy him. I know that you have the power of the little man over the big and you are determined to use it. However," she released the clutch pedal, reversing slowly so that Henry was forced to move out of the way, "I once had some considerable influence over Professor Ellis. Maybe it is not too late to revive it."

She turned the car round slowly and began moving down the long drive. At the top she slowed down, leaning out of the window. "Whatever happens, Felix will be looked after. He is the descendant of Shakespeare and he does have his own dreams."

She drove back along the twisting, narrow lanes, down Rumbold Hill where in the last century starving children had grovelled for crusts and back to the safety of her own home.

Later, as she fell asleep beside the snoring, restless body of her husband, she thought briefly, achingly, of her own baby — a full term child, perfectly formed but stillborn.

'Fifty years ago,' thought Frances calmly. She moved closer to her husband.

"Ardie," she whispered, "are you awake? We may have sort of adopted a child. His name's Felix."

R. D. Davendish slumbered on.

THE JOURNAL OF GILBERT SHAKESPEARE

DECEMBER 1582

Tannakin tells me with an anxious look that she thinks she bears my child. Now am I truly repaid for loving too well and must be tormented on earth as well as in hell. Whatever else may happen, she must be protected and though some would judge her harshly as a faithless wife yet do I know he deserves to be deceived and feel no guilt or shame. I ask the lady gently if she is sure the child is mine, wondering if there might be occasion for persuading Oxford that the deed is his, for I care not if my child be passed off as his so long as Tannakin suffers not. She replies with hesitation and with blushing cheek the babe is mine, for Oxford, though he lies with her in duty bound, does fall asleep most nights in drunken stupor and never knows what deed is done.

I rejoice most gladly and say "Persuade him that the child is his, if he will believe it!" but she trembles at the thought, remembering how Oxford on returning from his travels, had accused her wildly and without cause of making him a cuckold, forcing her to live apart for years, her reputation shamed. She is convinced deception now will be revealed and men will see the child and know the truth, and though I say "New babes are all alike and none can guess the fatherhood," yet she cries "And as it grows each passing day we'll live in fear in case the resemblance proves too strong."

And I suppose her reasoning is right, for if the child should inherit my deformity then none would doubt. Though I think that God is not so cruel as to inflict such suffering on an innocent child, yet is she convinced He will as punishment for her guilt, for she alas does suffer torment and calls herself adulteress and a whore, though saying through her tears she loves me still. As I do her and though I do regret my love should lead to her grieving, yet am I proud with a secret and most fearful joy that she should bear my child.

So the deed is all arranged and she will tell her lord she is with child and he can think his duty is all done. Then shall I make arrangement that the child be born in secrecy and she shall say the babe is dead by being born too soon, but God be with me and the living child shall be smuggled far away under night's dark veil and raised elsewhere.

Tannakin is much relieved and seems content to leave the plans to me and only glad that Oxford will not know the truth for she fears his anger and his drunken cruelty too much. I wonder how she will feel when the babe is born and taken from her, neither dead nor living to her, and my heart is torn from me when I consider how she who I adore must suffer for my deed.

In heaviness must I away to Warwickshire for I need help in the planning of these dreadful acts and it seems most fitting that the family who cast me off those years ago and left me as a destitute, should be the ones for taking part in deeds that would make the angels weep.

Oh Tannakin why has this come to pass? That such a night of love must bring us the hours of dark despair. You raised me high in love and now am I bringing you so low.

'WHAT'S DONE IS DONE'

Frances, on her way to meet Ellis, felt sick with nerves. It wasn't the thought of seeing the man who had meant so much to her; she had long ago learned to bury irrelevant feelings. Annual meetings and the occasional letter, for all that Ardie's paranoia saw them as more, were little more than faint ripples on the surface of a deep, silent lake. Frances felt sick because she realised this meeting could be the most important one she had ever kept.

She walked slowly down the Causeway, once lined with tall trees, where Queen Elizabeth had ridden on her seven day visit to Cowdray House. Frances could almost hear the slow groaning wheels of six hundred carts laden with trunks, each one dragged by six weary horses, their hot flanks steaming and their breath making patterns in the bright air.

'What a woman,' she thought, 'trailing court and crown all over the land to save herself money.' She considered Elizabeth, who had walked a tightrope of nerves every day of her life, fending off plot and counter plot, treachery and fear. Had it taken its toll of her? History offered tantalising snatches of weeping and passion, of screaming rages and near hysteria, but the overall pattern was one of control.

'What would she do?' thought Frances, crunching the golden brown leaves underfoot. 'What would she say, how would she handle Ellis?'

She saw Ellis as she came to the top of the Causeway and stopped to gaze at the magnificent view of the ruins. He was already inside the grounds, standing in front of the buildings on the eastern side, his dark-blue overcoat over his shoulders, staring thoughtfully at the ground. Behind him the great walls rose tall to the sky and the early November light shone like glass through the vast bay windows. From the outside this portion of the house appeared intact and beautiful. Inside it was all a shell, cursed to bitter destruction by a mad monk and devastated by a fire so fierce that the embers had smouldered for a fortnight. Ellis was not looking at anything.

'Wasted,' thought Frances, making her way through the gate.

"Hello Ellis," she said, standing right in front of him. He glanced at her and Frances thought a hint of pleasure flickered in his pale blue eyes. Then it was gone.

"Good afternoon, Frances," he said, looking at his watch. "I am glad the thought of keeping an appointment with me did not force you to hurry yourself in any way. I was looking at you ambling along that path as if you had all the time in the world. Star gazing as usual, I suppose?"

"Well," said Frances, "we may not have got all the time in the world, but there is no need to start counting seconds as soon as we meet."

"I have a business meeting in Godalming at six o'clock," said Ellis. "I can spare you one hour."

"Oh don't strain yourself!" said Frances. "We haven't met for over a year and you say you can spare me one hour!"

Ellis sighed. "I am a busy man, Frances. My time is very precious. You are your usual dramatic, mysterious self, summoning me all the way from London for a so-called urgent, private meeting. Fortunately I was able to tie this business in with another appointment. I have no objection to humouring you but I am curious to know what is so important that a telephone call would not suffice and we must meet in this desolate spot."

Frances counted slowly to ten. This was no way to begin. Queen Elizabeth would never have started a meeting with a head on collision like this. She glared at Ellis, standing there so cold and elegant.

"There are times when I really hate you," she muttered.

He laughed then, looking down at her angry face. "No, you don't." He paused and studied her. "You look tired, Frances. You shouldn't go racing around like you do, tearing yourself apart with emotion. It's not good for you."

"There are a lot of things that aren't good for me," she said. "I haven't got time to worry about them. I'm busy too, Ellis. Being busy keeps me alive."

"What can I do for you, Frances. I really do only have an hour I'm afraid."

"Let's walk round for a bit. I'm not ready to talk yet, Timmy. Please let me get round to it in my own way."

He shrugged. "As you wish. And please don't call me Timmy. You know it annoys me."

She glanced up at him. "You didn't mind once. When everyone else at Cambridge called you Ellis, I was the only one allowed to call you Timmy."

"For heaven's sake, Frances," he said. "I'm not in the mood to go down memory lane with you today. Let's get on with the business."

"I've never known you in such a bad mood. Whatever is the matter with you? I've seen you on television being successful so, if it's not that, it must be something to do with the Shakespeare Monument and your secret little schemes for opening it up!"

Ellis turned and stared at her, his pale blue eyes very cold.

"You never cease to amaze me, Frances. I suppose it's no good asking how in the name of heaven you know about that little project?"

"I have my spies," she said. "You're not the only one with informers, Ellis."

"So I see," he said.

Frances stroked her fingers across the old grey stone of the inner ruins. "This room used to be the Great Hall." She looked up at the open sky. "There were eleven carvings of stags on the walls."

"I've read the guide book too," he said.

Frances looked thoughtfully at her long time friend. "Please tell me about it, Ellis. I really do want to know about the Monument. There's been nothing in the papers so I suppose you can't have found anything new, but I'd still like to know about it." She moved closer, touching his arm gently. "I can see it was a terrible disappointment to you. I may have my spies," she added, "but I never pass on any of my information to Ardie."

Ellis flinched. "How is your husband?" he muttered.

"The same as ever."

"The same as ever," he repeated flatly.

"Tell me about the Monument, Ellis."

He groaned. "You do go on! Thank heavens I never married you. You would have talked me to death — I know, I know," he added as Frances opened her mouth to speak, "I meant thank heavens you never married me. I know you were the one who did the choosing."

"I'm not sure choice came into it. I needed a father for my child. Ardie offered immediately, with no hesitation or thought of his career or anything. You stood back and waited and watched. Weren't prepared to take the risk for all you pretended to act broken-hearted afterwards. Couldn't have any real involvement for T. Townsend Ellis, could we?"

"I really don't want to go down memory lane, Frances. It's too dangerous. It can't do any good. It was all so long ago."

She paused. "Tell me about the Shakespeare Monument, Ellis."

They stood there in the ruins of the ravaged house, glaring at each other in a silent battle of wills.

"It was fearful," said Ellis. "Like something out of a murder mystery. You know the sort of thing: when they exhume the body in the dead of night and there're arc lamps all around and a tarpaulin covering something and it's cold and grey and you know there's something terrible down there and any minute you might see it …"

"'And cursed be he that moves my bones,'" she said, thinking of the words carved on William Shakespeare's grave. "That's probably what spooked you, Ellis, the thought of an

167

ancient curse lying in wait for you, following you like a shadow."

He pulled his dark-blue greatcoat round himself. The air was thick with the smell of bonfires and a grey mist was rising slowly from the damp fields around the Causeway.

"But you weren't really disturbing his bones, were you?" asked Frances. "Surely you were examining the Monument, not opening the grave itself."

"We X-rayed the Monument. We were so convinced we would find some original manuscripts or something inside, written in Oxford's hand. So much evidence pointed that way. We know the Monument was tampered with in the early days; the original engravings are nothing like that idiotic bust on show today — and the inscription, it's always seemed so important to me, Frances. 'Read if thou canst, whom envious death has placed within this monument. Shakespeare.' The Monument is too small for a man's body to be placed inside! It must mean there's something else there: the documents, the proof.'

Frances looked thoughtfully at Ellis. His pale blue eyes were glowing with a fierce, passionate light.

"And what is there? What did your X-ray show?"

The light died. "Nothing," he said. "It was empty. We read the clues wrong. Looked in the wrong place."

"Or maybe it's your theory that's wrong. You've always been so sure that Oxford is the author but you could be wrong, Ellis, even you. Maybe you've got the right bit of the jigsaw but you're looking at it the wrong way round."

"Now we're getting there. This is what it's all been leading up to, isn't it Frances? You want to know how much I've uncovered about Ardie's latest precious theory."

Frances took a deep breath. For a moment the ground under her feet seemed to be swaying.

"I've no doubt, Ellis, that your spies have told you everything. You must know that Ardie is presenting his findings next month at Cambridge."

Ellis looked down at her in mock surprise. "Is he? I wonder what findings they are."

"Don't play games with me, Ellis. It's too late for that. You've been in contact with Henry Shakspeare, haven't you? Lots of times I'm sure. He's made no secret of his double dealing. You must know everything there is to know about Gilbert Shakespeare."

"Everything and more," he said.

There was silence. In the distance a dog was howling mournfully. Frances felt herself shaking.

"Yes," she said, gritting her teeth to stop them chattering, "I always thought there was more. Some revelation that will bring Ardie down."

She looked at Ellis and her eyes were bright with tears.

"Isn't it true then? Is it all a lie — those journals — are we the ones who have read the clues wrong?"

Ellis shook his head, trying to hide a small, triumphant smile. "No. Reluctant as I am to let my claim on Oxford go, I am beginning to think that Ardie is right about everything. The evidence he has collected may prove that Gilbert Shakespeare was the author of the plays and sonnets and that his descendants come directly from his love affair with Anne Cecil. There are a few background checks I need to do."

The ground stopped rocking.

"Then what more is there?" asked Frances.

Ellis looked at her almost pityingly. "You can't expect me to tell you that, my dear. You don't imagine Ardie would tell me, do you?"

"Why must you be such rivals?" said Frances. "All this plotting and secrecy and double dealing. It's shabby and pathetic and you can't see it, either of you. You're so twisted up with spite and envy!"

She walked up and down, scuffing the leaves. "Why can't you combine on this one? Get together for once and bury your differences. Heaven knows it's about the most exciting bit of research ever! Pool your findings and present them to the world as the contribution of two great and wise scholars." She grabbed Ellis by the wrist and he stepped back in alarm. "All this fighting, this determination to be first past the post, the winner, the one with the scoop! Call yourselves scholars! Gutter press, that's what you are. A gutter press mentality in literature's name."

She took a deep breath. Rooks in the tall trees cawed loudly. Across the fields a bonfire blazed and a firework shot over the greying sky. Ellis stood unmoving in the shadows of the old house.

"You're two old men," said Frances, her back aching with exhaustion, "two old men at death's door, fighting over a dead man to make yourselves a living reputation."

Silence.

"Have you finished?" asked Ellis.

She peered through the gloom at his face. "I've done it all wrong, haven't I? Said too much as usual. I've only one thing to ask you, Ellis, and then I've finished. I'll never bother you again. Ever." She gazed up at the man she had once loved desperately.

"What is it, Frances?"

"I am asking you not to use this information to harm Ardie in any way. Let him have his moment of glory, Ellis, be generous to him. I beg you, for the sake of the friends you once were, let him present his findings in Cambridge without cutting him up. You can write a book next year, Ellis. Have your moment of triumph then."

He shook his head before she had even finished speaking.

"You are asking the impossible. I cannot stand back in silence. I cannot wait till next year. I am an old man, Frances, and I cannot wait."

"Ellis," she said, her voice cracking, "I beg you."

He shook his head again, stepping into the shadows. "I must be going."

"Ellis," she screamed, "you owe me this! Have you forgotten? You owe me this one thing to make up … to make up for the …" She broke down sobbing and covered her face with her hands.

He moved slowly back to her side. Very gently he touched her grey hair.

"To make up for what, Frances? For life? I cannot do that. Whatever you may think of me I do not want to hurt you. You have always been the best person I have ever known. But you cannot bind me with the past. The past is dead and gone and all I have to live for is this chance of outwitting Ardie. The scoop, as you put it. It's him or me and you know he would say the same. This time, my dearest Frances, it is going to be me."

THE LEGEND OF THE LADY

(Chapter in a book on 'Ghosts of Warwickshire' written in 1940)

There is a tale, still told around these parts, of a lady of high rank at the time of Elizabeth in the strangest of circumstances.

This was a time when the land round about was thick with forests with a rich black soil and an abundance of blossom and wild flowers. It was a wealthy land, with beasts and vegetation and woods and stone and seams of iron and coal and salt as valuable as gold and rivers bursting with salmon and trout and grayling and eel. It had been known as a land of fertility and promise since the time of the Romans, with camps enclosed for husbandry, exporting much corn to the Rhine Valley, just as in 1549, a few years before the Lady of our tale was born, such corn was sent in abundance to starving Bristol. It was also a land known to poets, famous for its flowers and nightingales, where children followed the hare from an early age and learned the lore of angling and knew the signs of every season. It was a land thick with castles and stories of kings and pageants and murder on the battlements and miracle plays in the bright streets of Coventry.

Into this fertile country, men poured yet more wealth and built great houses and bridges and many a yeoman farmer made profit as well and built himself a magpie cottage, half timbered and strong to this day. Yet it was also a land of danger and fear, for these were the years of deadly plague and sudden fires, where often the Severn and the Avon swelled in flood and overran the towns, sweeping all before them.

But most of all it was a land of blossom and fruit, widely known and praised. Here Saint Augustine drank deeply of his favourite cider and William of Malmesbury wrote in praise of the neighbouring vineyards. Also from here, the men of Worcestershire, setting out bravely for distant Agincourt, wore their device of a pear tree laden with fruit. In this small stretch of land were a hundred sorts of vine, such as the Blood Red and the d'Aubois, more than forty kinds of plum and seventy types of apples whose names were chanted by local children as a sort of litany — the Underleaf, the Foxwhelp, The Magdalen and the Go-No-Further. Here the Paradise Apple grew wild as if in Eden again, while the bright sun in a blue, summer sky peeped and flickered and darted and danced above thick, white, blossom clouds in the Vale of Evesham. Here the whole land swelled with new life and here, secretly, one May night, to a small farmhouse in the hills, came the Lady of our tale, heavy with child.

In those days many goblins and fairies, witches and wizards, lived deep in the woods along with fugitives, hermits and robbers, so that charms, talismans, rhymes, chants and secret herbal potions were as normal as breathing. The midwife, who had been sent for hastily in the dead of night, shook her head doubtfully when summoned and muttered 'A May baby's sickly. You can try, but you'll never rear it.' However she was persuaded by the messenger pressing a heavy purse into her hands. 'There will be more,' he whispered, 'brought here on this date for every year of your life, but none must ever know the truth of this night's events.' The midwife nodded, her eyes glinting at the gold, and was impatient to be gone but the messenger held her tightly by the wrist and twisted it until she cried out in pain. 'If you should tell,' he said, 'even though it but be to the shadows, a knife will slit your throat that very night.'

The midwife shook in her shoes but stood her ground bravely. 'Why do you so delay me?' she exclaimed. 'Do you want the child born before midnight with none there? If we can but hold the pains an hour or so till dawn it will be best, for men do say the earlier the hour the longer the life.'

On entering the household the midwife unlocked all bolts and loosened the knots on her clothing according to custom, to give the Lady an easier birth. Then she muttered a rhyme well known in these parts:

There are four corners to her bed,
Four angels at her head,
Matthew, Mark, Luke and John
God bless the bed that she lies on.

The Lady was lying on the bed moaning softly. No-one else was in the room except a figure in the shadows. 'Out with you at once,' said the midwife brusquely, 'This is no place for boys.'

'I must stay with my Lady,' said the figure in the corner.

'Gilbert,' whispered the woman on the bed, 'there is no need to stay. I am in good hands.'

The midwife saw the boy's face for the first time. He was a young man of about eighteen. 'If you would help,' she snapped, 'go get a bowl of water with plenty of salt to bathe the infant when he comes, and he shall taste it three times for his health. Go.'

The young man hurried out. 'Now,' said the midwife to the Lady, wiping the sweat from her brow and stroking back her long hair, 'it will be soon, I think. First let me determine the sex …' She pulled a ring, tied to a length of ribbon, out of her pocket and held it high in the air over the woman's swollen body. It swung backwards and forwards very slowly. 'Good. It will be a boy. When the ring moves to and fro thus it is the sign of a fair boy.' For the first time the girl on the bed smiled. 'I have always longed for a boy.'

About one hour later the young man waiting impatiently downstairs heard the loud cry of a new born baby and bounded up the stairs and into the chamber before the midwife could stop him. The girl on the bed, white with exhaustion and soaked in sweat struggled to sit up. 'It is a boy,' she cried, trying to reach his hand, 'God has given us a boy!'

The midwife stepped forward angrily. 'Get out! Do you wish to make her feverish? I must cut the cord to show the length of the penis for his manhood and this is no place for you. If you would be useful,' she yelled after the boy, 'go gather the sap of the ash tree for the infant to drink and drive Satan and the witches away.'

As the young man let himself out of the house again to search for an ash, he heard his Lady sobbing in an upstairs room. 'They will take him away, my lovely son. They will take him away.'

That is what happened. That is what they did, so the story goes. Two days later, the baby, a strong healthy child, was collected by a man and a woman, both with their faces covered, and taken away by them in a coach. Rumour has it that the child was taken to Stratford and grew up there but I do not know the origin of this story or whether there is any truth in it.

The same day — and this is the strangest part of the tale — the Lady, dressed in black and weeping as if her heart would break, left in a coach for an unknown destination. With her she took a tiny coffin, sealed up, with a large stone wrapped up inside. The messenger, who had travelled with her, was sent ahead with the instructions 'Tell the Earl his son is dead at two days.' More was said but unfortunately has not come down to us.

And that is the end of the legend, except that on May 9 each year, round about dawn, there have been many reports of a figure in black seen near the site of the old farmhouse, and if you listen carefully you may hear something which you think is the wind in the trees, but there is no wind. It is the sound of a deep, deep sigh.

JOURNAL OF GILBERT SHAKESPEARE

MAY 1583

In this month was born my son to the sweet lady whose name I dare not speak, nor ever acknowledge the child as mine.

My brother William and his wife, for a great fee, have taken the boy to rear as their own; my brother's wife having recently given birth to a daughter and willing to suckle both.

The word was voiced abroad that my Lady was delivered early of the Earl's son whilst journeying in Warwickshire, being taken too soon by her pains to travel back to London, and that the boy did die at two days being sickly.

The Earl is much cast down for he thought the child was his, the heir for which he has so long hoped, and so had him interred, or so he thought, with ceremony and bitter tears at Heddingham. So has that, of which he did most wrongly accuse my Lady, come to pass and he is cuckolded at the last and so serve all cruel husbands.

My brother sends word that the child is well which news I did whisper to my Lady, but she turned her face away and wept most piteously for that she does long so for the tiny boy.

Satan and his devils could create no worse hell than this.

JOURNAL OF GILBERT SHAKESPEARE

JUNE 1588

And so my Tannakin you are gone from me. May God and all his angels keep you safe throughout eternity. Men say there is no weeping there so your unhappiness is at an end though mine is but begun.

They wrapped you in a winding sheet and draped the rooms in black cloth and the staircase too, and laid you in a casket with yew and rosemary for death and remembrance. With choirmen singing solemnly and one hundred fine horses all in black they laid you in your noble grave attended by many persons of great quality, my Lady Mary and my Lord John de Vere being also in attendance.

The Earl did act as though deeply grieved but I did note no tear upon his cheek, though my lord your father did weep as if much afflicted.

And I, who loved you most in secret and forbidden love, must stand in silence with bowed respectful head as one who was a servant though my heart breaks and I would howl in torment.

Here comes my brother William with a secret plan for making his own fortune here in London. Now does he hear reports of how my scribblings are performed and praised and has discovered how men say that fame must be the prize of one who conjures words and weaves enchantment with their spell. None but he have guessed that I, a servant born of humble stock, mocked and ill regarded, could ever be the author sought throughout the court. For many try to tease out truth and rumours spread more wildly than a flame, but I will guard this secret as closely as the rest. I remember how it gave my Lady private joy to pass my scribblings from hand to hand in ways so twisted and so tangled up the court itself became a maze. But I am as turned to stone and I am lost.

My brother William does demand that I shall write and say the credit is all his and he the author. He thinks to make his name or else cast out my son of five years old to be a beggar in the streets as I was, until my Lady Anne did rescue me to be her tumbling boy.

He does threaten like a man gone wild to tell the world the truth and drag her name upon the mire as wanton and a whore and so he would. For though he may appear to many as a gentle man with no ambition for himself — and so he seemed to me when I begged him in the name of brotherly duty for his help with our sweet child — I hear he chafes upon the bit of marriage with a shrewish wife and in need of fortune longs to leave behind the bridle paths of Warwickshire and turn his face to fame and London life.

Let him have the plays, the poems, I care not, my heart so sick that any words I write henceforth will be as letters scribed with my heart's blood and so I say do as you will but guard the name of Lady Anne as if it were your life and keep my son until he be a man and takes the dealing with the world upon himself.

And at the last, when none did see, I tossed sweet herbs gathered at the dawning hour upon your grave, for herbs that bear the cold dew of the night are strewings fit for graves.

'HIS ONION STONE'

The room was very quiet as Ardie rose to his feet, making a show of adjusting his spectacles.

"Ladies and Gentlemen, I am honoured to be here today. First of all because this historic town of Cambridge has been for so many years the centre of my life. It has been the heart of my intellect, my senses and my understanding. In the old streets outside I learned to think, along the river banks in the days of my youth, I learned to feel; in your famous chapels and ancient buildings I learned to understand and here, within these walls, I learned to apply. In this place first grew the seed that today has come to fruition."

He gazed slowly round the room. "I am honoured by the presence here today of so many colleagues and experts in their fields. Without their work, I should not be standing here. They are the ones who have laid the foundations and it is with gratitude that I honour them."

The silence in the room was absolute. Frances, sitting near the window by the platform, glanced round and saw respectful, admiring faces. The place was intense with expectation. It was as if an old shire horse, put out to graze, had felt a quickening in his hooves, a scent of greener grass. Ellis, on the opposite side at the back of the room, careful not to catch Frances's eye, nodded in Ardie's direction, acknowledging the tributes. Of Henry there was no sign.

"Shakespeare," said Ardie slowly, "and you will note I give him as yet no Christian name, is an everyman. He is a man beyond time, a universal voice, the heart of our confused and

182

troubled world. He has something to say to everyone, whether it be to the child taking part in his first school performance or the scholar whose brain is teeming with cross references. He is complete. Yet he is faceless. We know what he may have felt but we do not know what he looked like. We don't even know who he really was. It is as if a being from another world appeared one day in ours, wrote volume after volume of work and vanished again. A genie, a will o' the wisp, an alien from outer space — it could as well be any of those as any man we know about. Until today that is."

Frances felt her heart pounding with the tension in the room. Ardie wiped his face with a handkerchief. "The mystery of Shakespeare has fascinated people for generations. People have always felt that somewhere, somehow, there were letters, diaries, references that would bring all the threads of information together. For years I have feared that all this documentation must be lost, not meant for our eyes. However, amazingly, it does exist. It has come to light.

"Ladies and Gentlemen, I cannot tell you how honoured I feel that these treasures should come to me, that I am the one with the magical key to unlock the most marvellous story chest ever known. My friends and colleagues here today, I ask nothing more of you than your attention, your total open mindedness and utter rejection of any preconceived ideas. My friends, I want you all to come on a journey with me, a challenging journey because change of any kind is unsettling, but nevertheless a breathtaking journey. I want to tell you a story. A story that has waited too long for the telling. The story of Gilbert Shakespeare."

Frances found that she was holding her breath. The heat in the room was unbearable. She rested her throbbing head against the windowpane and noticed, with surprise, that it was snowing heavily outside. At the back of the room someone turned the lights on and people blinked irritably, unwilling to break the spell of Ardie's words. Frances watched as two figures, one tall and one short, bending low against the wind, stumbled across the dark courtyard.

'It's going to be alright,' she told herself, watching the attentive faces round her. 'They're all with him. He is really going to make it this time.' She put her hands in the pocket of her long, grey raincoat, her fingers rustling on a letter. 'I've made it,' she thought with a thrill of joy, touching the letter again like a talisman. At last a publisher was willing to publish her book, in her name, with her photograph on the back and no strings attached. 'I'll tell Ardie tonight,' she thought. 'He'll be so excited by today's triumph that he won't mind too much. Please God it will all come right for us at last.'

The old door at the back of the room creaked open slowly and all heads turned. Henry Shakspeare, wet with snow, crept in pulling Felix behind him. Ardie glanced up, paused briefly then carried on as if the interruption had not occurred. Frances saw Ellis watching the newcomers carefully. Felix was smiling happily up at the rafters, oblivious to the snow dripping down his fringe. His dark eyes looked enormous and his lashes were wet. The room was now full of draughts, as if the chill of the winter air had come into the room with the newcomers. Outside in the courtyard the snow had already filled in their footsteps. Frances shivered.

Ardie had been talking for half an hour and his voice was growing husky. He was talking about Anne Cecil and her bastard baby smuggled away at two days old into the depths of Warwickshire.

'And she never saw him again,' thought Frances. Tears trickled down her cheeks and she wiped them away fiercely. 'Foolish old woman,' she told herself.

"And so," said Ardie, shuffling through his papers searching for a missing sheet, tantalising his audience who was still hanging on his every word, "we come to the years after 1588, the years that I call an end and a beginning. They were an end because Anne, Gilbert's Tannakin, died. Aged thirty-one. Wrapped in a winding sheet and given a magnificent burial and her lover dared not even weep. Except in his lonely room. They were an end because William Shakespeare of Stratford, whom history has venerated as great, showed himself to be the greatest blackmailer the world has ever known." Ardie banged the table, making people jump.

"What did he do, this fraud, this blackmailer? He demanded payment for his part in hushing up the scandal. His payment, ladies and gentlemen? Fame was his payment! Everything that Gilbert Shakespeare had ever written or would ever write was to be in his brother's name. All credit and fortune to be his. And the threat? What threat did our precious William Shakespeare make? If the agreement was not kept, the child would be cast out in the streets as a beggar and the name of Anne Cecil de Vere, tormented beyond the grave, be publicly blackened!"

The room hummed with agitation. This was an attack against a god, a calumny too far. George Clarke, Director of Shakespearian Studies at King's, who was chairing the proceedings, cleared his throat, preparing to restore order. People stood up, calling out questions, demanding Ardie's attention.

"This is ridiculous," muttered an elderly academic who had been dozing at the back of the room. He staggered to his feet. "Call this research? How dare you!"

"Utter piffle," said another in a loud voice to anyone who'd listen. "Hundreds of people down the ages can't all be wrong!"

"Professor, when did you last visit Stratford?" This in a sarcastic tone from a woman whose two volume biography of William Shakespeare was in the non-fiction best seller list. "Every tree, every stone resonates with his heart, his vision! He must be weeping in his grave at your slanderous lies!"

"Madam," said Ardie, "I acknowledge your concerns and those of every single person in the room. This must seem outrageous to many of you. I confess myself appalled at the idea of William Shakespeare as a blackguard, a fallible idol with feet of clay. But truth will out. All I ask is you hear me a while longer. There is more to tell. There will be all the time in the world later for calm and rational contemplation of every issue."

He is magnificent, thought Frances, as the audience rumbled into grudging silence. She rested her burning head against the icy window glass, her jaw aching with tension.

"Those years after 1588," continued Ardie, "that I have referred to as an end, were also the years of a beginning. For in those years, Gilbert Shakespeare, knowing that he had lost forever the only woman he could love, knowing that his marvellous genius must forever remain unacknowledged and be accredited to another, in those years he wrote the plays that we call great. You will understand why these masterpieces, these words that speak to all men, are so full of heartache, of suffering, of eternal torment! Ladies and Gentlemen," shouted Ardie, banging the table and growing crimson in the face, "we owe it to this man to restore his name! He has waited four hundred years without an identity. He has been cheated out of his rightful place as a genius. If we let today pass without recognising the truth, then everything we stand for will be a lie!"

Frances felt the room growing black and clutched someone's arm in panic. As she opened her eyes slowly, she saw Ellis in his corner at the back: silent, watchful.

"Ladies and Gentlemen," gasped Ardie, "Mr Clarke, friends and colleagues, please hear me out. Original documents are securely locked away but facsimiles are here for your perusal afterwards. I have one more thing to say — possibly the most important of all."

The room quietened slightly. Ardie gulped down a tumbler of water as Frances watched anxiously. Felix, smiling to himself, was drawing patterns on the misted window pane. "My friends," said Ardie huskily, "Gilbert Shakespeare is dead. We shall make what amends we can but the grave is infinite. However, there are some to whom we can make reparation.

Here. I am speaking of his descendants who are standing in this very room amongst us."

He held up his hand to check the disorder that again threatened. At the back of the room Ellis laughed.

"I have been guilty," said Ardie, "of not giving credit where credit is due. I have been so overwhelmed by the revelations that have thundered upon me over the past few months that I have failed to acknowledge the assistance of the man who bears the blood of Shakespeare in his veins. The opportunity of putting this to rights I owe to my dear wife, without whose support I could not endure." He paused and smiled at Frances. "The time for making reparation to the man who is the descendant of Gilbert Shakespeare and Anne Cecil de Vere is now!"

He gestured across the room at Henry who was standing by the door as if rooted to the spot. "Ladies and Gentlemen, will you please give honour to Mr Henry Shakspeare and his son Felix, of whose existence I only recently became aware." Ardie's eyes were shining at his own magnanimity as he revelled in the role of patron.

"Mr Clarke, may I have your permission to introduce this gentleman? Mr Henry Shakspeare, come forward, come forward! Come and take your rightful place next to me on this platform where everyone may see you."

All heads were turning to look at the young man and the boy. Some who were sitting without a clear view stood up. Henry, his arm round Felix, moved forward as if in a trance.

"Welcome, you proud descendants of Shakespeare," cried Ardie, beaming at the pair as they stood awkwardly at the edge of the platform.

"I never thought you'd be so generous, Professor," muttered Henry. Frances thought how nervous he looked, overwhelmed by the occasion, not at all excited.

"Mr Clarke," said Ardie to the Director of Studies, "May we bend the rules of protocol once more? With your permission I would like to invite my wife to join me on this platform."

"Very well," said the Director. "On this occasion, as a matter of courtesy to your wife."

Frances reluctantly made her way to the edge of the group. Felix smiled at her and moved closer as the audience settled back in their seats, quiet and expectant.

"Ladies and Gentlemen," said Ellis in a loud voice from his corner of the room. "I would be glad of your attention." He made his way towards the rostrum, the focus of all eyes.

"Mr Clarke," he said, "may I have your permission to address this meeting?"

George Clarke, looking harassed, nodded his head.

"My colleagues," said Ellis, joining the group on the platform, "I would like to add a few things to today's proceedings. It has been a day of hysteria and I would like to add the voice of common sense. The voice of reason and of logic."

"What do you think you're doing?" said Ardie. "Who said you could get up and spout rubbish?"

"Professor," said George Clarke, tapping his pencil on the rostrum, "this is an open discussion. Please respect it."

"Ladies and Gentlemen," continued Ellis, ignoring Ardie's interruption, "we have before us a tangled web of fact and falsehood, truth and fiction. With deference to the full weight of your authority and knowledge in academic and intellectual matters, I will confront the Janus of truth, make him acknowledge you all face to face with his validity."

"Words, words, words," muttered Ardie, red in the face, furiously shuffling his papers on the table.

"Let me begin," said Ellis, "by explaining how I have become entangled in this web. You may say that I have no part in this story, there is no need for my involvement. Let me assure you that I have been drawn in thread by thread by one who most foolishly mistook me for a fly."

Henry, who had his arm protectively round his son on the far edge of the group, stared, white faced, at Ellis.

"I refer to this gentleman on my left for whom far reaching claims are being made. Mr Henry Shakspeare — for so he calls himself — has chosen to consult me at every stage of this fantasia, despite the fact that until recently he was in the employment of Professor Davendish. Furthermore he has entrusted me, behind our worthy Professor's back, with what he says is the final piece of evidence in his case. This he expects to be the trump card in his pack."

He placed a pile of papers on the table, gently nudging Ardie's notes to one side, and leafed through them slowly, enjoying the tension, taking his time. Henry's eyes were glittering and his face was damp.

"Here," said Ellis, finding what he was looking for, "I have a facsimile of a letter purporting to be written by Anne Cecil de Vere on her deathbed to the young man who had grown up in the Burghley household as her tumbling boy. This letter," he glanced triumphantly at Ardie, "reveals the fact that this person, who gives himself the name of Gilbert Shakespeare, was ideally suited to the role of tumbler for he was small. Even as a man he was always of low stature. He was, ladies and gentlemen, what used to be termed a dwarf."

Frances felt the room shake around her.

"Rubbish!" yelled Ardie, thumping the table with his fist. "Lies! A farrago of lies! No way was Shakespeare a dwarf!"

"You may ask, my colleagues," went on Ellis, smiling to himself and holding up his hand to stem the flow of words, "why this piece of information, leaving aside the issue of truth, should be offered to me by Mr Henry Shakspeare rather than to Professor Davendish who has been privy to all other letters and journals. The reason is obvious; you have heard the Professor's words yourself: he is appalled at the very idea of Shakespeare's genius being housed in a less than perfect frame. Henry Shakspeare realised this very early on. He chose not to have his precious secret sullied with such prejudice and so he came to me, knowing how I would trust the compassion and wisdom of people such as yourselves to take these facts, if they should prove to be true, to evaluate them without preconception or bias, to assess them with the dignity of honourable men."

Frances found herself shivering in spite of the heat. Ardie, stunned into silence for the moment, was rubbing his hand backwards and forwards across his forehead. A restless, uneasy audience tried to adjust to the concept of itself as compassionate, honourable men. Henry watched Ellis.

"There have been many words tossed around this room today." Ellis poured himself some water. "I need to add in a few more but believe me they are pertinent. I have a reputation for scholarly, painstaking research. Unlike some in our present company, I do not believe in rushing in ahead of the angels." He looked pointedly at Ardie. "I propose to break this web that would trap us all in delusion — note how carefully I use the word delusion. No more fine or foolish words; the time has come for facts."

He paused, making sure he had total attention. "To begin: Mr Henry Pettifer — for that is his real name, not Shakspeare, though a man may call himself by any title till he is challenged for the proof — Mr Henry Pettifer has walked the boards of theatre land for years. The original attendant lord, he has never made a fortune, known but little fame."

Frances felt a small hand creep into hers. Startled, she saw Felix smiling up at her. Gently, she squeezed back.

"For years this man has lived a life inside his head: intrigue, conspiracy, romance — more drama than even the famous Bard himself could think of. The stuff of fantasy and dreams to hide the details of his real life in some obscurity."

Frances felt Felix's hand pulled roughly away from hers. Henry, shaking his head violently, stumbled off the platform, shoved his way through the crowd that blocked the door and pushed his son out ahead of him. Snowflakes flurried into the room as the door slammed shut.

"Frances," whispered Ardie, "I'm ill. Take me home."

"You may ask," continued Ellis raising his voice above the clamour, "how did this Shakespearian delusion begin, how did these Tudor documents come into this man's hand, at what point did illusion become real? Will we ever really know the total truth? Now, be attentive for there is yet another delusion. Possibly the most important one, since the originals of some of these documents do exist and may be verified as authentic. If we do not expose them for what they are, then who knows but in the future some other misguided professor may topple headfirst into a pit."

Ellis smiled at his own wit and the audience, glad of a break in the tension, laughed too. Ardie's face was turning a pale green and he swayed on his feet. Frances looked round for help.

"Anne Cecil de Vere had a most unhappy life," said Ellis. "Married to the Earl of Oxford, her childhood sweetheart, her marriage turned sour. Discarded and slandered by the man she loved, her good name a sham, she was forced to smile and smile again, to turn a blind eye to his cruelties, to live a broken life. Does she, in death, deserve her reputation to be shattered again by this nonentity who calls himself Gilbert Shakespeare, whose erotic fantasies and megalomania are thrust on us today? I say a very sick mind has invented this delusion. I say shame on you, wretched upstart tumbling boy, go rot in your own grave."

Ardie, shaking and grey, collapsed into the chair behind him. Frances bent over, cradling him.

"Well done, Ellis," she said. "You have finally killed us all."

In many ways that was the end of the story of this bitter feud. Tears, words, the conclusion of things; a shroud of snow that fell from a wintry sky.

Some months later, when a subdued Ardie was beginning to recover from the shock of the night and order his household about again, Frances started writing another book.

'You were probably right about my novel,' she wrote to her agent James. 'I've packed it away in a box. It would hurt Ardie too much and I need to look after him. This one is about Browning. I'm sure you will approve. It is a study of the poem and issues arising from The Bishop Orders his Tomb at St Praxed's Church. A poem about envy. I am quite taken with the idea of two rivals competing for the best tomb, the best lapis or onion stone marble, keeping an eye on each other throughout eternity in case one gets the better of the other. I suppose there are people like that? Who knows?'

And what about Henry? Imposter? Genuine? Deluded? Real? One curt letter came to Frances from an address in Ely, demanding the return of any facsimiles still in her possession.

'I have nothing but contempt for the lot of you,' said the note. 'Truth will out. I am in contact with some important people in the States who are keen to hear more about my ancestor. You will all see.'

And Ellis? He had his moment of triumph in Cambridge but later, when he looked around, the room felt empty. Although he might have interviews and appearances to come, there was no-one to share the excitement with that night, and he had a sinking feeling in the pit of his stomach that the people who really mattered, Ardie and Frances, would break all contact with him for ever. Not everyone was impressed by the style of his intervention, regarding him as mean-spirited in his putting down of Ardie.

"There's ways of doing things, you know," someone muttered at him on the way out. "Call yourself a scholar?" Ellis felt chilled in a wash of contempt.

He made his way slowly through the streets of Cambridge. Shadows lurked in doorways and under bridges. He was terribly afraid of meeting one face to face.

Perhaps it wasn't the end of the story, because there was still the copy of the letter which Ellis clutched, unread at the meeting. Perhaps the day will come when someone might discover it again and claim it as another scoop. Or when the safe box is opened and the original of the letter, flimsy and time worn, is finally revealed. The letter that may be the missing bit of the jigsaw, the last thread of the web, the final words of the curse, the dying flame of the fire, the glitter of a dragonfly's wing seen out of the corner of one's eye, the final shape of a shadow. Whatever. Call it what you will. Words are the greatest deceivers of all.

LETTER FROM ANNE DE VERE TO GILBERT SHAKESPEARE

JUNE 1588

Seventeen summers gone since the day I saw you first, a child
of seven screaming at an imaginary dragon, ragged and wide
eyed with terror. I took you under my protection and gave you
my heart and you in return gave me yours and from that day
to this nothing has changed, save only the love between us has
grown deeper as you have grown to be a man, my Gillyflower.

Now the shadows grow longer and my days are numbered
though I know you weep to hear me say so, but at the last I
am not afraid, for God is merciful and understanding and will,
I think, pardon me for loving you too much, for if love be a
sin beyond redemption then would the world be better for all
men sinning so. In truth I am weary and would rest, though
not too long for eternity is an endless time and I would see
you again someday.

I do weep at nights at the thought of leaving you and my
dear father and mother who were always the best of parents
though my marriage to the Earl did give them so much grief
and disappointment. And my little girls — my sweet
Elizabeth, too long cast off, rejected by her father through the
years of calumny and spite, though now he does declare he
loves her well — and Bridget, and my baby Susan, those
precious later fruits of duty's joyless union — I am sad to
leave them, praying that their father will still care for them for

though daughters they could yet make good marriages one day, bringing Oxford joy and ease of mind.

I do beg that you forgive the Earl, my Gillyflower, for though you hide your hatred from me yet your eyes burn so with anger at his name and I know you feel the injuries he has done me as to yourself. Yet, if he but knew it, you have done him far more wrong by bringing out in me such warmth and passion as he has never known could be in me.

Though the world would be amazed and talk most shocked to think a Countess should lie down beside a dwarf and reach the heights and depths of passion, yet was it so. For what do appearances matter when devotion and belief are there, when feeling is much more than poor deformity, when love out balances the foolish idle talk of envious gossip? So though you be but small of stature and all your life some men may scorn, know that you have a mind and spirit that is greater than the world and a Countess did most truly love you and is ashamed she was afraid to tell the world.

And our poor boy, my Gillyflower, what of him? My son for whom I ache with longing every waking moment and in my dreams as well though five sad years are passed since he was mine to cherish for an hour. I pray your brother and his wife will care for him as for their own, and though I never met them I think they must have loving hearts to do so kind a thing and send my deepest thanks through you. I pray he grows to be a man with children of his own and their line in turn be proud of both our names.

Now one more thing before they make my winding sheet, for I fear with some despair that you will break your heart when I am gone and never more do scribblings, as you call them, for men to read and act and sing. And this is my last request of you, that you do not let your gift be buried with my body but continue for my sake, draining life down to the dregs though bitter they may be, for I believe you are a rare man and the world must know it too.

So now the light is fading and I long to rest. May God bless you and give us a long line of our descendants. May the world be such a place that they one day are proud to tell our tale.

Weep not at my grave. Throw sweet herbs that are wet with dew not tears. I know you will remember me.